Uptight New York writer Jack Christie inherits his uncle's estate including a small publishing house he never knew Cameron Christie owned. Among Cameron's papers are the deed to an old house on the remote island of Molokai — they call it the last Hawaiian Island — and a court summons. Cameron is being sued by relatives of one of the last remaining survivors of the former leper colony, Kalaupapa.

Cameron published a journal sent to him by the man who relatives say could not have written the book since he does not have the use of his hands and is senile. In an effort to hold onto the small amount of money that he's inherited, his uncle's hard-earned business, not to mention Cameron's reputation, Jack reluctantly travels to Molokai to solve the mystery. This shut-down New Yorker encounters more than he bargained for on this island shaped by myth and magic.

He meets an island man who could be straight out of his dreams. And Jack, who has always managed to keep his emotions under control, isn't sure he's ready to fall for a hot, sexy Molokai Man.

Molokai Man
Copyright © 2021 A.J. Llewellyn
ISBN: 978-1-4874-3402-1
Cover art by 978-1-4874-3403-8

Published by eXtasy Books Inc

Look for us online at:
www.eXtasybooks.com

MOLOKAI MAN

BY

A.J. LLEWELLYN

DEDICATION

To the memory of Queen Ka'ahumanu, whose gracious presence is so keenly felt on Molokai, and to George Helm, the original Molokai Man. Thank you for your tireless conservation efforts. And to Saint Damien of Molokai, father of the forsaken.

Warmest love, not forgotten xxx

CHAPTER ONE

October 24.

Jack's eyelids snapped open. His heart was pounding. Though he was still in bed, he was someplace else. His hand shook as he moved it to his mouth.

Impossible . . . it couldn't be . . . *my face is wet.* He'd dreamed of walking through a rainforest, following a tall, dark man, and it had started to rain. *Oh, no . . . now I'm hearing the dream. I'm hearing my footsteps . . . I can still feel the rain on my face!* He glanced around furtively. In the darkened bedroom, he saw the familiar shapes of his closet, dresser, the curtain against his window. His breathing was ragged. What a weird dream.

"How much did I drink last night?" he muttered aloud, turning toward the wall.

God, last night had been so depressing. He tried not to close his eyes, afraid the dream would be there again, sucking him in. He swore it was real. He could reach out and push back the suffocating jungle he found himself in. He could feel the leaves, smell the dense, cloying heat. *No, no, this can't be happening.*

He fought the green, tasting his fear on his tongue, aware of the other man, his skin warm, turning to him. The man started to speak.

"Please don't," Jack said aloud, and awoke once again to find his hands stretched out in front of him, groping. For what? He concentrated on breathing. Who was the man? He

1

focused on the city sounds. Yes . . . yes. For once he was grateful for the old Pinto his neighbor spent hours revving each morning before dawn. It was a familiar sound. It grounded him.

His thoughts drifted back to the dream. *The jungle. Man . . . too much green.*

Green was not a common thing in New York City, and certainly not here, not in the heart of Hell's Kitchen, sorry, Clinton, as the real estate agents, and his boyfriend Robert insisted on calling the gentrified neighborhood.

Jack forced himself out of bed, despite his usual hankering for sleep. He was afraid to close his eyes because, as ridiculous as it seemed, he knew the dream would still be there. Even now, the peculiar birdsong of the jungle was still in his ears.

"Stop!" he shouted. He swung his feet to the floor. It was early. Seven o'clock in the morning. Too early for the pounding of jackhammers that started as if on cue outside his brownstone on the corner of Ninth Avenue and Thirty Ninth. It competed with the loud, irritating thump of techno, now bursting from Wanda's stereo. He almost called the dominatrix who lived upstairs, but thought better of dealing with her histrionics, and padded to his bedroom window.

Brushing the curtain aside, he stared out of the cold, grimy window at the apartment buildings and ritzy boutiques that had displaced the mom and pop restaurants, cafés, even a great bookstore.

New York's coldest late fall on record had brought misery and a huge drop in business for everyone . . . except Wanda. The cops had been here again last night, interviewing her. What a mess. She was a wild one all right. Somebody had reported screams from her second floor apartment. It hadn't been Jack who reported her, he'd been out with Robert, but he knew she would assume it was him. He sighed. Wanda was a nightmare on her good days. On her bad days, she was terrifying.

Jack blamed Robert for his bleak circumstances. Robert had said this was the best street in the fast-developing gayborhood. In Jack's opinion, this was failing upward. He'd wanted to move to Christopher Street. Too gay, Robert insisted. *But I am gay.* Poor Robert, he was so deeply entrenched in his closet he'd never find the door.

Should I try calling him again? Things had ended awkwardly between them last night, but it hadn't started out that way.

Jack dropped the curtain. The first floor apartment he'd bought just two months ago shook with the force of the work outside. The music upstairs suddenly stopped, making Jack dizzy. Then, it started again.

"This is music?" he muttered to himself, turning on the thermostat, relieved when it groaned into gear. Since the roadwork had started, he'd twice lost all power, his gas, water, telephone . . . and now it was thirty-one degrees in the big city.

He trotted to the kitchen to make coffee and opened the gas oven, ramping up the heat.

Last night. The date had started with a bang. An amazing dinner at Molyvos, a lovely, romantic meal for two he'd carefully ordered ahead. He and Robert shared a love of the Greek Islands and Jack had thought this beautiful place might revive happy memories for Robert. Jack had been worried about the endless construction on Seventh Avenue but things had been fine. Jack had chosen day-boat sea scallops, and juicy and tender grilled baby octopus served with lemon, olives and fennel. They had lingered over oaky Macedonian red wine and the selection of spoon sweets he'd picked for dessert.

They'd finished with tiny cups of Turkish coffee and ouzo then Robert got that gleam of desire in his eyes Jack hadn't seen for weeks. They walked the sixteen blocks back to Clinton and he let Robert hold court once more, hoping beyond hope for a happy ending to a wonderful evening.

As Jack looked back on all their dates, he realized alcohol tended to make Robert a bit . . . pompous. In fact, a fake British accent tended to slip out. Last night, there was just truth. "I know I've finally hit my stride," Robert said. "I'm forty-two. I'm not just a late bloomer . . . I'm a miracle man."

Jack had laughed. Robert was, as he liked to call him, his silver fox. Prematurely gray, he had a great smile, wonderful personality, and a body that belied the long hours he spent online and on the phone, checking listings and drumming up sales. He'd been a child star who'd taken his drop into obscurity very hard. He still had the talent and the looks that were a sharp contrast to Jack's black Irish ancestry. At thirty, Jack knew he wasn't ugly, just frustrated with his career, which unlike Robert's, was not on the ascent. It wasn't going downhill either. It was just stagnant.

They had passed the gated entry to a British teashop that in Jack's recent memory, had never been open. Robert had reached for Jack's coat collar, silently pulled him into the unlocked entryway, pressing him against the cold window, which displayed a white, garden tea party service strewn with fake, green ivy.

Their mouths met with an urgency Jack thought he'd never feel from Robert again. The kiss didn't last long, and Jack was surprised to taste oregano on Robert's tongue. It was as if his body didn't want to forget the meal they'd shared. Robert backed away from him and stepped out onto the street again. He was aroused, and when he got that way, he could often be critical.

"Did you contact the Manor agency?" he asked as they fell into step once again.

Jack had to clear his mind of erotic haziness. "I did . . . I emailed my resume, even tried calling. Never got a call back."

Robert's lips thinned as if it were Jack's fault that an

obscure job lead Robert had found on Craigslist turned out to be a dud.

"Things aren't moving for you, are they?"

Jack was a little taken aback. As usual, he tried to joke his way out of responding to one of Robert's barbs. "If things move any slower for me, they'll rust." He instantly regretted it. Robert didn't have much time for Jack's frustrations with his writing career.

"You're a great adman, Jack. Forget about the other stuff."

No, I'm not. I hate it. I did one good campaign that got me a decent payday . . . and led me to you. I am not a great adman . . . and the other stuff is my writing. It's my life. Jack bit his lip to avoid saying this aloud, to avert a show of anger.

"It's for lunatics and dreamers . . . or the very rich. You're no dilettante. Concentrate on making money."

Instead of saying anything he thought might lead to an argument, Jack launched instead into what he thought was an amusing anecdote about a rejection letter he'd received from a big publisher . . . addressed to someone else.

"So, not only do I have to deal with my own rejections, but somebody else's as well," Jack quipped, only to be cut down by his lover.

"I don't understand why you keep submitting stories and books to publishers only to be beaten down."

Jack didn't see it that way. He didn't know how to respond. They arrived at his pad, only to find Wanda screaming at the cops out front.

Robert glanced at him, looking mortified. "I'll call you." He touched Jack's hand briefly, turned on his heel and headed back uptown.

You snob! Jack wanted to scream. He felt bereft, especially after the hefty dinner tab . . . not to mention how long it had taken to coax Robert into meeting him in the first place. Since Jack had bought his apartment, he'd seen less and less of Robert, who always seemed to be working. A surprise visit to his office when he was allegedly doing so one night, embarrassed them both because he really was working late. And now . . . he didn't know what to think. Robert had been reluctant to see him again after that horrible encounter.

"I need a man who's a little more secure," he told Jack, who up until he'd met Robert didn't think he was insecure.

"And I need a man who wants to be with me, who wants to spend time with me. If you don't want to do this, Robert, just tell me. Let's do it, or not do it . . . not both."

Robert had relented, agreeing to see him. Jack had cleaned the apartment because Robert was so fastidious. Now, Jack felt for sure, Robert was seeing another man. He'd been too quick to run off last night. So why didn't he come right out and say so, instead of making Jack feel like such an ass for pursuing him?

He assembled his thoughts, staring down at the stove. The water was taking its time boiling . . . and he sighed. He spooned freshly ground French roast into his new French press. The old one had shattered the day before, when an unexpected burst of hammering out front knocked it clean off the counter.

The kitchen, which needed a tremendous amount of work from tile replacement to a new stove and new plumbing, was perpetually grubby because of the street repairs. No matter what he did, dirt and dust settled like a new skin each day.

His phone rang and for a heartbeat, his breath quickened, hoping it was Robert.

A low, gravelly voice. "Hello, Jack Christie?"

"Yes." *Please don't be selling me long distance phone service or a homeowner's warranty plan.*

"This is George Sullivan. I'm—"

"George. I didn't recognize your voice."

"I'm your Uncle Cameron's attorney."

Attorney? Is that what we're calling long-term lovers these days? "Is everything okay, George?"

George sighed. "Look . . . there's no easy way of telling you this, but Cameron just died."

"Died?" Jack was in shock.

"Look . . . can you turn that hideous music down?"

"Sorry, it's not mine. It's the woman upstairs." Jack switched off the stove, and boiling water spilled everywhere. He carried the phone into the john, the quietest room in the apartment, since it backed onto an alley. "George . . . I'm so sorry. What happened?"

Jack's thoughts were spinning. Uncle Cameron was his only close relation, his parents having moved from Boston to New Zealand two years ago. Cameron and George had been together for years, but Uncle Cameron . . . well, he preferred to keep his private life to himself and hid behind a veneer of of carefully crafted, asexual respectability. Whenever Jack saw him, they usually had lunch at Zabar's Café on a weekday. On a few occasions, they'd met for late Sunday brunches at Caffé Reggio, the only remaining classic Greenwich Village café. Little Italy had vanished, like so many other neighborhoods. And now, Cameron was gone.

Jack had treasured their moments together. Cameron once let it slip that George was out of town, at the Cape with friends, and Jack sensed how lonely his uncle was without him.

The one time Jack suggested Cameron join his lover on vacation, he didn't hear from him for over a year. Cameron was like that. Despite Jack's entreaties, Cameron had cut him off. And then George had called. Jack tried hard to think how long ago that was, as George sobbed, unable to speak on the other end of the phone. He remembered now . . . late spring, almost a year ago.

Thanks to George's intervention and his advice not to expect an apology or to instigate a discussion on the ugly incident, Jack had gone to meet Cameron and George for lunch at their apartment on Waverly Place. He'd even taken Robert, at that time his new lover, though neither George nor Cameron seemed to like him.

Their contact with Jack had been sporadic since Cameron had kidney issues last year. The two men had become remote, often not returning calls for days, sometimes weeks.

"He . . . he . . ." George's voice broke. "You should know it was an accident. He slipped and fell in the bathtub. Problem is . . . the hospital wants to donate some of his organs and you'll need to come down here and sign these forms."

"You want me to do it? Why?"

"He left everything to you. You've inherited his entire estate. He . . ." George's voice still wobbled, but there was a bitterness to his tone now. "Yes. He left it all to you. The publishing house, the money . . . and . . . the lawsuit."

"What publishing house?" Jack's brain processed the last word. "Did you say lawsuit?"

"Please come down here. He's at Gouverneur Health on Madison."

Jack hung up the phone and walked numbly through his vibrating apartment. He had one leg in his thick, brown corduroy pants when a loud thumping noise outside rattled him. And then he heard a crash in the kitchen.

He ran to find the new French press shattered all over the floor.

CHAPTER TWO

Jack lived two miles from the hospital. It was faster by foot, even though he was freezing. His heavy black boots must have sprung a leak because his socks squelched as he took broad strides. He almost swooned with pleasure at the aroma of fresh, roasted chestnuts at a corner stand on icy Bleecker Street.

He turned onto Hudson, then onto Broadway, his breath coming in painful spurts as he cleared the last two blocks to Madison. The newish Gouverneur wasn't the amazing architectural paradise the old building was. The original, now a residence for the city's homeless, had seen changing fortunes as a hospital. The modern-day version was cutting edge, with a stop smoking clinic Uncle Cameron had championed.

In the lobby, Jack found George Sullivan in his pajamas, a stylish oilskin overcoat buttoned crookedly, one side of his collar up, pacing the hallway. Within seconds, they were in the hospital director's office.

"It was his wish to donate his organs." George looked dreadful as he held a leather folder in shaky hands on top of the director's desk. "I went home and retrieved Cameron's legal papers."

He paused and Jack wondered if he'd been drinking. *Or is he hung over from last night?*

"Found 'em. Hidden in a wall safe." George's voice dropped. "He changed it behind my back . . . look at this . . . Legalzoom.com. Can you believe it? Have you ever heard of such a treachery? *Thirty years* I was with that man and he

9

didn't trust me." He pushed the leather folder toward Jack and got to his feet. "Good luck to you."

"Wait . . ." Jack touched George's arm. "Please stay. This is awful. I'm sure he didn't know what he was doing . . ."

"Don't you say that. Don't you ever say such things about that man." George's whole body shook with rage and, Jack knew, shock and exhaustion.

I can't say anything right. Jack felt a strange sensation, the smell of leaves, something crossing his face. He shook his head. Man, that had been some dream last night.

He took George's arm, realizing for the first time, the proud lion was getting old. The two men accepted the director's offer of mint tea and declined transplant procedural counseling.

"Probate takes nine months to process in New York," George told Jack. "But since time is of the essence, you're going to need to agree to the organ donation now."

"Time *is* of the essence," the chief surgeon assured them. "We'd like to harvest his viable organs as soon as possible."

Harvest? He's not an apple tree! Jack stared at him. Some doctors had no bedside manners. This one had the finesse of a serial killer. Jack read and signed the papers, making sure George saw every page. He felt George was mollified somewhat by Jack's insistence that Cameron would have wanted this. Jack had to sign several papers . . . each for a different body part and recipient. For a moment, as he and George reached the page for corneal transplants, George fell apart again.

"I can't look at you, I can't," he shrieked. "Your eyes are just like his."

Jack glanced out the window. Snow fell lightly now . . . like sugar dust from the sky. Cameron always had had a sweet tooth. And, he'd always loved white winters. How inconsequential, Jack realized, his hand hovering. He was signing away his uncle's body parts. Nothing in his life had prepared him for this moment. He took a deep breath and scrawled his name on the last page, catching the hospital director glancing at the wall clock.

"Eighteen people die every day in this country waiting for organ donations," the man said.

Jack blinked. He swayed a bit. What an awful thing to say. Was he insinuating that Jack was taking so long, that one of those waiting might die?

"Would you like to say goodbye to him before we begin?" the director asked, as though realizing he'd been crass.

No. "Yes," Jack whispered. He and George walked along the squeaky-clean corridor of the cardiac arrest unit and paused at the open door.

All kinds of hospital workers and machines waited for the . . . harvest. Jack glanced at George's teary face. Thirty years and it had come to this, his waxen-faced lover lying in bed. It wasn't him anymore. Cameron was gone. Jack felt numb staring at the man on the bed. He couldn't touch him. It was too painful. He took George's thin arm.

"You had to go native!" George's voice oozed dark fury. He passed a hand across his brow. "Oh, Cameron. Have a nice sleep." His voice cracked.

"Can they have a minute alone?" Jack asked the hospital staff.

"No. I don't want to remember him like this." Tears fell down George's crumpled face.

"Let's go home, Georgie." Jack kept his voice gentle.

"I can't leave him here. They'll hurt him." George was hysterical. Out in the corridor, two nurses approached them. Jack was surprised how kind they were.

"Would you like a valium?" one of them asked him.

"I would like to die," was his response.

They organized a bed for him in a private room after a brief consultation with the ward doctor. He lay on his side as a young intern came in to give him a shot in the ass.

"Don't look," George attempted to smile at Jack. "He may be gone, but my ass still belongs to him."

Jack moved from the window, where he'd been watching the mad morning crowd on Madison and perched on the edge of the bed, holding George's hand. George relaxed within seconds. Man, that was fast-working stuff.

"He'll be asleep for a couple of hours. I can't release him unless you are taking him home," the intern whispered. "He needs to be accompanied by somebody."

Jack assured him he would do this, then asked, "Am I allowed to sign a release form for him?"

"We need the bed," came the intern's response. "And he didn't have surgery. Just . . . um, a tranquilizer."

"Sign it," George said, apparently awake. "Get on with it."

Jack signed yet another release form. When he was sure that George was really asleep, he moved to a chair by the window and braced himself before opening the zippered, leather folder.

Keystone Press. Unbelievable. His uncle had opened his own publishing house and so far, had ten pretty impressive published books to his credit. *All the years I've been struggling . . . he could have thrown me a bone.* Jack immediately chided himself. *No. Look at how he treated his lover . . . like an ugly secret.* Jack saw contracts with at least fourteen authors. There were bank statements, spreadsheets . . . two of the authors made decent money, the rest were not earning money even worth mentioning. One of the newly signed authors was a British cricket player. Uncle Cameron was a lifelong cricket fanatic who had gone to see England play at The Oval in London.

Then there was the letter. Oh, man . . . the letter. It was from the family of a man in . . . he mentally stumbled over the Hawaiian word *Kalaupapa*. Kah-loh-papa. Okay. Now what was going on there? The envelope was stapled to the hand-written note, postmarked Molokai. Jack knew this was a small, remote Hawaiian island. The letter, written by a man named Kalino Garcia Jr., stated that Cameron Christie had published a book that was a memoir of his father, Kalino Garcia Sr., one of the last remaining survivors of the former leper colony, Kalaupapa.

Per your letter of August ninth, my family is shocked that this book has been published since we have no record of this journal you allege was sent to you by my father. He could not have written this journal since he does not have the use of his hands and is senile. We demand that all copies of this book be destroyed, and a million dollars be paid to my family, or lawsuits will be flying . . .

Aloha to you, too. The family had indeed filed a lawsuit, but that didn't faze Jack. Anyone could file a lawsuit. What did upset him was that the book, a slim volume entitled *Molokai Man*, was written in diary form, its entries beginning in 1951. Could Kalino Garcia have been senile way back then? Jack thumbed through the book, determined to read it. There were photographs depicting Garcia, a strapping-looking Hawaiian man in various stages of evident good health and then crippling illness. Jack could hardly look at the handsome man's twisted, bulbous feet and hands.

Jack studied the black and white photos of patients who were lined up in front of houses . . . some of their faces chewed up by the disease. Leprosy—at the time of Garcia's banishment to Molokai it was not yet known as Hansen's Disease—had taken its toll. The photos were sad; glimpses of journal entries, devastating.

I stepped on a six-inch nail, but didn't feel it, even when it poked through the top of my foot . . .

What was missing from the file was the original journal. Clearly, Cameron had gotten hold of it somehow. He hadn't invented the man's existence.

Jack looked up to find George's glazed eyes focused on him.

"I want to go home, Jack. Please . . . I want to go home."

Jack helped George into the spacious, wonderfully decorated apartment he'd shared with Cameron all these years. It was huge by anybody's standards, and took up half a block on the corner of Waverly and Gay, the short street that connected Waverly Place to Christopher Street.

Jack thought about his first visit here when he was five, and all he could remember of that experience was books and music. His gaze went straight to the bookshelf on his right. The fourteen feet of books had dazzled him as a child and still did. Antique volumes collected from Cameron's travels all over the world. Next, his glance always went to the tiles on the entrance floor. Italian, hand-painted tiles in a star-shaped pattern from the seventeenth century.

Beyond this, the rest of the apartment boasted polished wooden floors Cameron had coveted as though they were living, breathing entities. Despite hours spent slaving over their sheen, he'd never asked people to remove their shoes. He thought it was rude.

To the left was Cameron's grand piano. As a child, Jack had seen it constantly in use, since at the time, Cameron had been a symphony orchestra pianist and songwriter. These days, sheet music was no longer piled on it and around it in random fashion. The lid was down. Jack had never seen it with the lid down.

He'd walked into a set designer's Shangri La. The entire, block-length apartment was filled with furniture from the nineteenth century. Cameron had a complete suite of furniture from the 1920s he'd bought from the former silent screen actress Nita Naldi, just hours before her death. There were original paintings from master artists, including a Gaugin once owned by Errol Flynn that Cameron had bought at auction when the actor went into bankruptcy. Speculation had swirled for decades over ownership of the piece, but Cameron preferred to keep his 'lips zipped,' as he liked to put it. He never publicly claimed ownership of any of his pieces, preferring to see the delighted shock on people's faces when they came to the apartment.

"It's all yours now," George muttered, waving his hand around. The very act caused him to stumble, and Jack led him to the sofa, easing him onto it.

"Can I get you something to drink?"

"You can stop treating me like an infant. We need to talk about the lawsuit." He heaved a sigh. "And the fact that he never told you he put your name on everything. Even *I* didn't know it."

Jack felt an odd, icy sensation scissor through him, and straightened. He noticed for the first time there were wet towels on the floor. George's head was back against the sofa, and Jack followed the wet trail into the bathroom. The shower curtain had been torn off its rings. Water still dripped from the tap in the bathtub. He stepped forward and turned it off. When he turned around, he caught a glimpse of himself in the mirror, and there was Cameron, staring at him from behind his shoulder.

Turning around, he realized he was imagining things. It was that dream. It had disturbed him. He walked back into the living room. George still sat there, arms limp, head lolling against the back of the sofa.

Jack watched him for a moment, opened the hall closet, retrieved a pillow and cashmere throw, removed George's shoes and laid him down on the sofa to rest.

George whimpered in his sleep, and Jack moved to the window seat, looking out at the gray, miserable day. The view from here never failed to lift his spirits. From here he could look down onto Christopher Park and George Segal's white bronze statues of a gay couple standing, and a lesbian couple seated on a park bench. These were strong symbols of gay pride for people in New York.

Jack loved this place, but it really belonged to George. Jack couldn't believe Cameron had left it to him. He longed to know how long his name had been listed as a co-owner. Wouldn't it have cropped up in an online search? Wouldn't Robert, the real estate bloodhound have discovered it? It wasn't fair. He hadn't seen anything in the file about the apartment being his, but George kept insisting.

He glanced at his uncle's longtime companion, who was sleeping quietly. He didn't snore like Cameron. Jack glanced at the leather folder and wondered again about the lawsuit.

"You know, we could lose it all."

Jack started. He whipped around. George was still lying down, but was looking up at him.

"Help me up. Goddamn valium. Get me a drink, will you?"

"Are you sure—"

"Oh, I'm sure. I'm not going anywhere." George started to cry again. "No. wait . . . I'll make us coffee."

Jack hated when George made coffee. It took him ten years, even though the results were always worth it. The man took forever to produce a single cup due to his overwhelming fastidiousness in the kitchen. Jack followed him into the large room. The couple's two dogs had died a few years ago, but their basket, with a plush blankie and a few soft toys, remained. George didn't look at it, but Jack glanced at it. He couldn't believe it was still there. He took a seat at the kitchen table. George only made coffee and drinks in the kitchen. He never cooked because it made too much mess. When he invited people to a meal, it was always prepared by a chef who delivered. Now Jack sat back and watched George indulge in his complicated coffee-making ritual.

"I suppose you're wondering about the lawsuit?"

"Of course I am. I read the letter from Mr. Garcia. Is there a journal in existence?"

George's hand stopped as he measured the coffee. "Not as such."

"What does that mean?"

"Your uncle was . . . having strange dreams."

Dreams? Jack started to sweat.

"Oh . . . it was weird, believe me. But then he found the man online. They corresponded . . . and then the journal arrived. Cameron photocopied everything, but the original is missing. Stolen from Cameron's office in Honolulu."

"He has, um, had, an office in Honolulu?" Jack was stunned. His uncle was such a New Yorker, he'd once freaked out at the notion of having to travel to Chicago for his best friend's wedding. He'd declined the invitation, wrecking a lifelong relationship. Apart from a long ago visit to Europe, Jack had no knowledge of Cameron leaving town. His head was spinning at the notion that Cameron had ever been to Hawaii. He had a million questions, but George's hand suddenly stopped in midair. He slumped to the floor. Jack rushed over to him, catching him. George's unfocused eyes opened again.

"I can't believe he's gone."

Jack held George for a moment, shocked at how fragile he felt. It was as if he were nothing but skin and bone.

"Help me up." He swatted at Jack's arms as he got to his feet again. "That bastard!" he shouted at the kitchen cupboard. "Goddamn. He bloody left me!" George turned to him. "I want to walk."

"Are you sure?" Jack blanched at the baleful stare from George, who had given up on making coffee.

"I can't do it," George whined. "I can't carry on with wifely duties. I'm too upset."

"Of course you are," Jack soothed.

George got to his unsteady feet and stumbled out. He even left the kitchen in disarray as he trotted to the bedroom to put on trousers.

The two men armed themselves against the inclement weather with scarves and thick gloves and took the elevator down to the lobby. George's red-rimmed eyes were pitiful. Jack took his arm as they left the elevator.

"People will talk. They'll say you're my toy boy," George said and giggled.

"They'll say I have excellent taste in older men," Jack responded, and the two men turned right, trudging the dirty, gray ice and melted snow-lined street.

"Not a winter wonderland," George sniffed. "We need to go to Bonsignour."

"We do?"

"Of course. It's Wednesday, they make their chicken fingers on Wednesday."

Jack smiled. These were—had been—Cameron's obsession. Jack was still grappling with thinking of Cameron in the past tense.

They walked in silence, except for the street noises, until they hit Jane Street.

"I think I saw his ghost in the bathroom," George suddenly said as they approached the tiny café with the green awning.

Jack wondered whether he should tell George he had seen his uncle, too. Something told him not to . . . an odd sensation that George needed to believe Cameron was still there for him only . . .

"Do you think it's weird?" George asked.

"No, I don't. I am sure he's still there."

George studied him for a second then switched gears as

they approached the wonderful neighborhood deli. "Oh look, Jack. A table's opened up."

Jack paused to inhale the fragrance of Bonsignour. It forever smelled of coffee and boasted the most lavish cakes Jack had ever seen. He tried to pull open the door, forgetting that it worked the other way.

"You always do that," George said with a chuckle. He raced to the newly empty table. This was a coup considering there were only three tables in the entire café. Jack was happy to sit, and allowed George to dominate with his ordering. Soon they were sharing warm, sliced turkey and brie on dense black bread, chicken fingers, thick chunks of chicken with beet salad on walnut raisin rolls, and endless cups of espresso as the unhappy lines of people lengthened outside.

The two men traded stories about Cameron. "Remember the time we went to London and he insisted on seeing that forsaken musical, *The Bounty*?" George shook his head.

"I enjoyed it." Jack grinned. "I liked the theater, Her Majesty's . . . it was . . . stunning. All that red velvet."

"Oh, my dear . . . have I taught you nothing? It was so tacky!" George shuddered then signaled for more chicken fingers. He loaded up the new Czech waitress with empty plates. "And bring us some cream cheese brownies while you're at it," he announced to her retreating back. George leaned forward. "Now . . . about the will."

"I don't want to discuss the will." Jack glanced around the crowded, tiny café.

"My dear . . . he left everything to you."

"So you said."

He held up his hand to ward off anything else Jack might say.

Jack ignored him. "I don't want it. It's yours. It's—"

"Do you also run red lights?" George asked. "A raised hand is a universally recognized stop sign." The waitress slapped down a plate with a single brownie on it and George stopped her with a red glare. "And what is that supposed to be?"

"Is . . . brownie." She looked flustered.

"Can we not have two? I assure you, I'm good for it."

She frowned. "Is all we have."

"How dreadful. We'll have rice pudding then."

She reached for the plate.

"Leave it!"

Jack wanted to die. He couldn't believe George was taking out his fury on the poor girl.

"No rice pudding," she said. It was a blatant lie, but Jack admired her attempts to stand up to him.

"I see some in the window, silly girl." George pointed at the showcase, and she walked away from them.

The brownie was very good. Jack however, was aware of the tension George was creating. Normally, he was the one smoothing Cameron's rough edges.

"He left the apartment to you with the provision that I'm to live there in perpetuity. Technically speaking, we're co-owners, but I can't lease it without your permission, and I can never sell it." There was a trace of resentment in his gaze. "He left a very detailed will. I can stay there forever and I am grateful for that."

"Thank God," Jack mumbled around the creamy middle of the brownie. "I wouldn't want it any other way."

"But I can't leave it to an old cat's home, or a young lover . . ." George smiled then. "But the business . . . that and the money are yours. I want you to manage things. By the way, you're going to have to handle them soon. Cameron was supposed to fly to Molokai this weekend."

"This weekend?" Jack felt like a fool, repeating everything George was saying, but all of this was a huge shock.

"He made plans to meet this man in Honolulu . . . another

publisher who has been acting as a mediator and who has come to know the family. You're going to have to go in Cameron's place. Naturally, the ticket transfer into your name will cost some money, but it's doable since we can prove he died. We can get you a bereavement ticket."

Jack said nothing. His mind was still spinning like a teacup ride at an amusement park.

George licked his fork. "Thank God there's a few dollars in the bank. These people mean business, Jack. They got some fancy lawyer on board." George frowned. "He's one of those people who has been representing native Hawaiian families in the homestead issue."

Homestead issue? Tired of parroting each shocking statement he heard, Jack pressed his lips together. He'd go online as soon as possible and research it. All of it.

"This goes back decades, centuries actually." George rubbed his top lip with an impatient gesture. "But basically, many native families all over the islands were robbed of their land and properties in unlawful rulings. Slowly but ever so surely, some of them have filed forms with the Hawaiian government to restore their right to the land. They have to prove *Kumu 'Ohana*, genealogy, and it's a very long process. This attorney is one of those men who is rabid, and I mean, like a demented pit bull when it comes to native Hawaiians and their rights."

Jack swallowed hard. Suddenly all the food he'd consumed hardened in his belly. How was he supposed to tackle something he knew nothing about?

"The Garcia family and the attorney don't seem to understand that the publishing business is not profitable . . . that this journal is . . . was . . . pretty much a vanity project."

George held up his empty coffee cup indicating his need for a refill and held up two fingers to the waitress. "I know he never offered you the chance to publish one of your books.

One day, you might understand. He thought the world of you. He just thought . . ." George sighed as the waitress approached them timidly with their rice puddings.

She took off as George started to order her around again.

"He thought what?" Jack really wanted to know.

George waved his hand, as though it were a pesky fly. "Anyway . . ." He dipped into his dish with his coffee spoon. "You have the same gifts your uncle does . . . did." He frowned. The rest of his face followed and he started to cry again. Jack hastily threw some notes on the table, mouthed sorry at the waitress and bundled George out of the café.

Jane Street was a snowy blur as he hailed a taxi, and he was surprised when one stopped within seconds. Another couple grasped futilely at the other passenger door as the driver took off with Jack and George barely installed in the back seat.

"You have his gift . . . with people . . . and taxis." George smiled through his tears. "People respond to you."

At the apartment on Christopher Street, George insisted on going inside alone. "I know we're co-owners, but I need some time to think."

"We're not co-owners. It's yours. I . . . I don't want to lose you now he's gone, George."

"You can't lose me. I'm too big to fall through your pockets and too old and ugly to toss in a dumpster." George kissed his cheek. "Call me to talk about your trip."

Jack had no intention of racing off to Hawaii. It was ridiculous . . . his belly was making strange noises as the taxi pulled up outside his building. He paid the driver and noticed with satisfaction that work on the street had been suspended due to the snowfall. He glanced at the building, admiring anew the Georgian period detail on the front of it.

He wanted to be here. He *needed* to be here. He was not giving up on Robert. Robert loved him and frequently said so. He walked up the stairs and into the building. He heard

Robert's laughter, and felt deep joy . . . but the laughter was coming from upstairs. He mounted the steps to the second floor, shocked to see Wanda, her robe open, revealing her hermaphrodite secrets, her penis and her boobies, and her trademark malicious smile as she lounged against her doorjamb.

"Fantastic, see you on Saturday, sweetheart," Robert said, zipping up his trousers. He dropped a kiss on her cheek, his gaze following hers.

Jack and Robert stared at each other.

"I can explain," Robert said as Jack ran from the building, Wanda's evil cackle burning into his brain.

CHAPTER THREE

"He's a bad egg," George said for the third time. "We couldn't *stand* him. Why do you think we stopped calling you? He hounded us to sell this place."

"Oh, George . . . I had no idea. Why didn't you tell me?"

George pushed a highball glass into his hands. Jack recognized a Pimm's punch when he sniffed one. It had been the first alcoholic drink he'd been allowed when he turned sixteen, the appropriate age Cameron deemed for a young man to appreciate a tipple.

Jack eased back on one sofa, sipping at the cocktail, as George hurled himself onto the other, putting his feet on the coffee table. Jack tried not to stare. It was strictly forbidden to put your feet on any table in Jack's family, especially *this* branch of the family. Cameron also preferred footwear at all times, and George was flexing his toes now, his brand new Argyle socks seeming to mock the former house rules. *Man, he's only been dead for six hours and all hell's running amok.*

Jack took a long pull of the Pimm's, savoring the bittersweet tang puckering against the inside of his mouth.

"He came here a few times, left postcards, mailed a few letters. Then he left cards with seeds . . . that was quite clever, considering his next deposit was actual flowers and a bloody plant, if you can believe it. Some sort of palm that arrived, infested with white fly. Another time, he sent Godiva chocolates, packed on dry ice, if you please."

Jack just stared, feeling bewildered as George bellowed. "It's sick! Unbelievable . . ." Jack began to wonder if he knew

24

Robert at all.

"We saw him walking down the street with a woman. I wanted to tell you, but Cameron insisted we shouldn't . . . especially when we realized it was a Shim."

Jack shot forward, almost spilling his drink. "You saw him with Wanda? I've lived on the floor below her for three months and never guessed she was a man."

George hesitated. "She was all over him, and he was embarrassed, and then I saw that she needed a shave. I wanted to bolt, but you know Cameron, he was fascinated. You know he *loves* to put people in awkward positions. He invited them up here. She was quite out of her depth, poor creature. Listened politely when Cameron raved about the pianist Yuja Wang. We'd just gone to see her at the Philharmonic. Then she asked Cameron if Yuja was any relation to Vera Wang!" He brayed like a horse.

Cameron and George were such cultural snobs they must have enjoyed her ignorance. Anguish skittered across George's features. "I still can't think of Cameron as gone."

Jack felt the bile rising in his throat, despite his empathy for George's loss. *You should have told me!* "So it became easier not to see me than to tell me the truth?"

George held up his glass. "Care for another?"

"I probably shouldn't."

"Yeah, like we both have boyfriends who need us sober." George's words hung between them like a shopworn dress on a wire hanger. He reached for Jack's glass and crossed over to the wet bar. The sound of ice cubes falling into glass was the only sound. Jack listened hard. The typical thrum of passing traffic was very remote . . . as if it was far off in the distance and not right outside the windows. The wonders of double-glazing. He wished he could unload his apartment. It would never feel like this to him . . . so quiet and safe . . . not now. Not after the sickening sight of his boyfriend visiting Wanda, the devilish dominatrix.

"How long do you think it's been going on?" George's voice invaded his thoughts and, once again, Jack was struck by how George seemed to always be able to read his mind.

"No idea." Jack accepted the drink and took a healthy swig. He started to laugh. "He never sent me chocolates . . . or flowers."

George smiled. "What about seeds? Did he ever give you those?"

"Only seeds of doubt." Jack could not believe he was getting hammered with George and it was only lunchtime.

"Ah. Did the penny ever drop before . . ." George waved his hand around. "Today?"

"I suspected there was somebody else. I didn't think it was Wanda. He couldn't take off fast enough last night when she was outside yelling at the cops."

"You and I seem to have a talent for attracting men addicted to disbelief," George said, crossing his feet on the coffee table again.

"That's an interesting way to put it." Jack mused on the words.

"Well, I did everything I could for thirty years . . . danced a merry tune for my man. Interesting that he could see that trait in you and couldn't stand it. Often you know the very thing that is a weakness in us becomes the thing we most despise in others."

Jack stared into his glass. How true it was . . . only he'd never thought about it like that. "Did Robert give up trying to get you to sell the place?"

George shot him a guilty glance. "We told him unless he backed off, we'd tell you about Wanda."

Jack tried to take this calmly. "So how long *do you* think it was going on?"

George didn't look at him. He reached beside him to pick

26

up a manila envelope. "I have no idea, angel. I suspect he's known her for a while. We did a little digging. She owns most of the apartments in the building where you live."

Jack shook his head. "No wonder nobody could do anything about the damned music."

"I hate to tell you this, but she's been selling off units, though some are rented. It's odd that he pushed you to move in there. He must have known you'd eventually find out."

"Not necessarily." It was starting to hit Jack, the realization that the man he thought he loved preferred a . . . person like that to him.

"Don't fret, honey, we all make mistakes. Look at me, I'm living proof." George lay back across the sofa, swinging his feet off the table. Jack reached across to catch his glass before the contents spilled all over the floor. Within seconds, George was sleeping. Jack sat for a moment, closing his eyes, intending to rest them.

Wanda was waiting for him with her open robe and mocking laughter.

It was early evening when Jack awoke. The apartment was dark. He could hear the faint noise of rushing cars and realized, as he sat up on the sofa, that there'd been no rainforest dream. He was greatly relieved. He couldn't have been experiencing the same dreams as Uncle Cameron, though. Surely?

He gasped. He could feel leaves . . . his hands were around a tree trunk now. His face went into the gossamer threads of . . . a spider's web. He hands fled to his face and he felt he couldn't breathe.

"Easy . . ." The voice . . . *Oh man, I heard that voice last night. It can't be. It's the man from my dream.*

"Jack, are you okay?" A light came on and George was sitting up ramrod straight on the sofa. "What is it?"

Jack was still stuck in the jungle, and he stared at the older man for a moment.

27

George was staring back at him. "Don't tell me you're getting them, too?" He stepped forward. "Wake up, Jack." He gripped him by the shoulders, shaking him hard.

Jack was fully present now. In the corner of his mind, the dream man retreated and Jack felt a peculiar sense of abandonment. He almost slapped himself. It wasn't the man in his dream who'd abandoned him. He'd lost his uncle, his closest living relative, and his lover, all in one day.

He felt the spider's web spinning around his head and kept turning to get out of it.

"Come on," George announced loudly. "Let's get dinner."

Once again they bundled themselves against the inclement weather, and once more they went downstairs and stood outside the building. Neither of them could face the city. Without a word, they turned and went back inside. They were in the elevator when Jack finally asked about the dreams.

"What did Uncle Cameron say about them?"

"He didn't say much. He saw—" George bit his lip as the elevator opened and the only other resident of their floor, whose apartment took up the other half of the small street block, was coming out of his front door. Jack recognized him as a movie actor; his smile was warm, though his attention was elsewhere. Jack glanced past the actor to his blaring TV. He was watching his own movies.

The actor left his garbage bag outside his door and, with a nod for George and Jack, closed the door again.

"He does that every night," George huffed. "Drives us nuts." Inside the apartment, he rifled his carefully ordered takeout menu pile. "How's Manting for you?"

Jack almost laughed again. It was the only place they ever ordered from. George didn't wait for a response. He must have had the restaurant's number on speed dial, and within fifteen minutes, they were at the dining table, opening up containers of hot chili chicken, pepper shell shrimp and a zesty shredded potato dish cooked in wonderful, rich sauces that had both men moaning with pleasure.

They opened a bottle of red wine, and on top of the Pimms they'd been drinking earlier, Jack was starting to feel heavy and pleasantly uncaring about everything. He knew George did not want to discuss Cameron's dreams. *Fine.* He sipped more wine.

"I am curious about Kalaupapa." Jack leaned on the table with both elbows. Normally, George would scream at him, but this time he, too, was slack in his table manners. As a five-year-old, Jack had been forced by Cameron to eat his first meal here with telephone books under both arms, so he would learn the proper way to eat like a gentleman. "I read something about the old leper colony in Hawaii, but that's all I remember. How did Uncle Cameron find out about the journal? Did he ever tell you?"

"He claims to have received a message online, even though the family says the old man doesn't type. Now, some of the emails are in my office . . . I will sort through everything. I just need a few days." George's eyes were reddening again.

"No hurry," Jack assured him.

"Oh, but there is a hurry. Cameron wants to be cremated and his ashes to be buried on Molokai, in the back garden of the house he bought there." He spiked a lone snow pea in the last remaining carton with a chopstick. "You now own that, of course."

"A house on Molokai? He bought a house there?"

"That's where the dreams started. He says he felt alive again there. He . . ." George paused and drew a deep breath. "He fell in love there."

Jack couldn't believe what he was hearing. "What are you talking about? He was in love with you!"

"My dear boy, we loved each other. I'm not saying it was an open relationship, but sometimes things happen. He didn't fall in love with a real man . . . it was some . . . imaginary lover."

For a moment, Jack became aware of the man in his dream. Could he possibly be dreaming the same things as his uncle? "You're joking," he said aloud, more frightened now of his dreams than he'd ever been afraid of anything.

"No, I'm not." George sighed. "You're not as fanciful as your uncle. You won't get carried away with the mystery, the myth of that island. Your uncle might love . . ." He caught himself. " Might have loved me, Jack, but not enough to make our relationship public. Not enough to . . ." His glance went to the leather folder still sitting on the coffee table.

Jack didn't say anything. He sensed George's utter despair. There was nothing he could say to make him feel better.

"Anyway, I know you're not tied down to a full time job, and it's not like you have that rat fink to worry about," George said. "This is the perfect time for you to go to Hawaii."

"You're coming too, right?"

"Oh, no. I'll send you his ashes. I'm furious as all hell that he changed his burial plans. We bought a plot together at Calgary Cemetery. Now look what he's done."

"Has the hospital given you any idea when . . . you know . . . they might release him?"

Cameron wiped his eyes with the back of his hands. "When I got back after our little excursion this morning, they called to say the . . . um . . . harvesting procedures went well. Cameron changed the lives of six lucky people today."

"That's pretty amazing," Jack said. "I'm glad to hear that."

George nodded. "I'm supposed to call tomorrow to find out exactly when they'll release the . . . uh . . . remains."

"Oh, Georgie . . ." Jack rushed over to hug him, and for a moment, the older man caved into his wallowing grief. He pushed Jack away and snatched up his wineglass again. "You can do this for me, right, Jack?"

"Yes. Can you do me a favor while I'm away?"

"Anything," George said, his eyes bright with unshed tears.

"Find a realtor and help me get rid of my apartment. I never want to live there again."

George nodded. "Delighted to help. Now I have a new project. I *need* one. Tomorrow, I'll find all the papers you need for your trip. And that damned house key. It's around here some place."

"You think I should stay there?" Jack asked doubtfully.

"It's a small island, Jack. There are a couple of hotels, but I have to admit, the house has a certain . . . rustic charm. You'll like it. Who knows . . . maybe the ghost won't bother you."

Jack stared at him. *I think he already is bothering me . . .*

CHAPTER FOUR

Jack spent the next two nights in the guest room in the apartment on Christopher Street. He was spared any more rainforest encounters, and happily put them down to the shock and a few too many cocktails. He went back to his place once, to pack a few essentials. There were no messages from Robert, no notes. He felt relief, even as he wrestled with the painful stab of rejection. He hurried back to Christopher Street. He loved the bedroom, which had been his own since the age of five. For twenty-five years, Cameron had kept his things in there.

Saturday morning, as he awoke, aware he was due to fly out of La Guardia for Los Angeles in a few scant hours, he roused himself up and out of bed.

He had the peculiar feeling he would never see or touch his childhood possessions again. He moved over to the wooden bookshelves George had erected for him. He touched the Darth Vader Collectors' Case that still held his *Star Wars* action figures. They were now probably worth a fortune . . . there was also his X Wing Starfighter. He'd loved that thing. He smiled at the Transformers dolls. His Megatron and Optimus Prime had been his favorites. They took him to another world . . . a happy, wonderful world, where he could be powerful . . .

Growing up, Cameron had been his refuge. However prickly he'd been about his own sexuality, when Jack realized at the age of fourteen that he himself was gay, it had been

Cameron who'd helped him tell his parents. His mother cried, but his father apparently had already guessed.

"I knew it," he said, slapping his thigh. "I've never known a teenager not wanting to pinch his dad's girlie magazines!"

"Dad," Jack, the budding writer had deadpanned. "I wouldn't mind reading the articles."

His relationship with his parents worsened over the next couple of years and he spent weekends with Cameron, who could no longer hide his relationship with George. The two men were wonderful to him when he came home from bad dates. They educated him on clothing, conversation and dating etiquette. He resented weeknights with his parents, who still tried setting him up on dates with girls. There had been one girl . . . Eliza. She was a pistol and turned out to be gay also. She remained his dearest friend for years until she was killed in Tower Two in the 9/11 attacks.

Jack turned his back on his bedroom. It would still be here. Only Cameron was gone, not his entire world.

In the kitchen, George was sobbing. The sound devastating . . . wretched . . . and Jack padded into it softly, astonished to find papers strewn everywhere.

"He left me, Jack! What the hell am I supposed to do now?"

"Come with me." Jack waited a beat and repeated his words.

"I can't."

"Why not?"

George paused. "I . . . am so afraid I'll never see him again. I catch glimpses of him, you know. Does that sound crazy?"

Jack kept his voice tender. "No, George. I saw him, too. In the bathroom."

Eyes bright, red nose twitching like a rabbit's, George looked at him. "Have you seen him lately?"

"No," Jack admitted. "George . . . come with. Listen, you said he loved that place . . . Molokai. Perhaps he's waiting for you. A friend of mine lost her mother and a medium told her to think of her as being in another room. That's all death is. Our loved ones are just waiting for us in another room." He paused. "What if he's waiting in that garden?"

George's eyes reddened even more. "You're a wonderful man, Jack. What a glorious thing to say . . . but I simply cannot pack in anything less than three hours."

"Try. I'm going home to get some stuff. I'll pick you up in a taxi on my way through. You have two hours. Come on, ol' man. Where's your spirit of adventure?"

"I'm not old. Watch yourself, bucko."

"Two hours, Georgie. Be ready."

"What if I can't get a ticket on the same flight?"

"Then we'll fly out later."

He left the apartment, feeling better already about his journey. He and George would muddle through together. He walked down the street and received a shock. A for sale sign on a building, whose apartments he'd always coveted. Number fifteen had once been the Oscar Wilde Bookshop, a forty-two-year-old landmark and one of the original gay bastions of Christopher Street, not to mention New York as a whole. It had closed down several years ago and been replaced by a high-end clothing store, then a drycleaner's, then a day spa. Now it was a letterpress and stationery store.

Jack could still recall the sad white banner pasted across the shop window. To him and Cameron, it had been a cold, hard slap. *We do not have the resources to weather the current economic crisis and will be closing our doors for the last time on March Nine, 2009.* There was also a quote from Wilde. *There is no truth comparable to sorrow. There are times when Sorrow seems to me to be the only truth.*

Things were changing in New York . . . too fast. He studied the For Sale sign. It was one of the upstairs apartments. Jack raced over to the box of real estate leaflets and shook out one of the soggy pages. He could give George another project. Get him an apartment in this building. Oh, no. He stared at the price tag. *Fourteen million dollars! Get outta here!*

He had no idea what Cameron had left him but he was certain that between the inheritance, his own savings, and the sale of his apartment, the combined funds would not get him an apartment on Christopher Street. A sudden flash of rain and forest flickered in his mind. He blinked. Man, he was never going to drink another cocktail as long as he lived. The day was even more dismal than the previous ones. Last night, George had told him Hawaii's weather would be balmy. *Balmy! I'd like a bit of that.*

Jack grabbed a cab uptown and found, when he arrived at his apartment building, that it was still standing. He was stunned as he let himself into his unit, to find Robert hot on his tail.

"We need to talk."

Jack sighed. "Robert . . ." He detected the strong odor of Scotch on Robert's breath. Reluctantly, he allowed him into the apartment as he started to pack his things. He didn't want Robert in there, but it was better than the neighbors listening to their conversation. As if on cue, the music started from upstairs, and a look of disgust crossed Robert's face.

"How can you put up with that?"

Jack laughed. "You're joking, right? All the time you spend up there, you've never heard it?"

"I don't spend that much time . . ." Robert began weakly, and the music level increased a notch.

Outside, the jackhammering started. Robert turned white. "This goes on every day?"

Jack shrugged. "I told you before."

"What a dump."

Jack wheeled on Robert in fury. "You talked me into this dump. Surely you knew? Or have you only been screwing her since I moved in here?"

Robert was starting to sweat, and he stuck two fingers

under his shirt collar. "Cripes, it's not so bad when you're up there. And I can usually talk her into turning it off."

"Of course. Money talks."

Robert's faced turned red. "Look, I really can explain."

"You think so?" Jack took out his black, fake leather Kenneth Cole Reaction suitcase, the best thing he'd ever bought on eBay. He flipped it open and started piling in shirts, jeans, tennis shoes, a couple of blank notebooks, and some clean underwear and socks.

"Where are you going?" Robert asked.

"Just going away for a few days."

"I heard about Cameron. I'm sorry."

Jack didn't respond. He knew he couldn't carry anything liquid weighing over three ounces on the plane, thanks to the post 9/11 regulations, but he had a phobia about not being able to clean his teeth several times a day. There was nothing he could do. He would purchase a travel toothbrush and tube of paste at a convenience stall at the airport once he'd cleared security—if they confiscated his large tube. Robert was babbling as Jack threw more toiletries into a small bag and tossed it into the suitcase. He paused, retrieving his work notebooks and tipped them into his laptop bag with his computer.

It occured to him that he had nothing suitable to wear to or on an island. What did people wear in paradise? *Maybe I need to buy some T-shirts and jeans.* He put a couple of pairs of jeans and an open-necked T-shirt and a couple of long-sleeved shirts into his bag.

Robert's voice droned like a gnat circling against his ear, and Jack closed his suitcase, surprised at how clear-headed he'd been in his packing. He knew his cord pants, thick cable sweater and overcoat were most unsuitable for Hawaii. *I don't have time to shop right now.* He checked his watch. Twenty minutes. Technically speaking, he had some time before he was due to collect George. Maybe even enough time to grab something for his trip. Regardless, he wanted to be away from this apartment, the awful music and his blathering ex-lover.

"So . . ." Robert was saying when he finally tuned into his monologue. "What do you think? Would George be interested in selling it now?"

"Get out," Jack said. "Before I call the police."

He staggered down the hall with his suitcase, and felt he could breathe again once he got outside the building. It took all his reserves of will not to toss his house key into the gutter.

"Call me when you get back," Robert shouted after him.

"Don't hold your breath," he screamed back, startling a pigeon on a barren tree branch. The shouting did him some good. He wheeled his suitcase over the slushy, icy street and down the block. He checked over his shoulder, but Robert wasn't there. Jack's hands and face burned from the cold. He'd forgotten his coat. He hailed a taxi and blinked. His uncle Cameron was standing across the street smiling at him. He blinked again. *Gone.*

Jack asked the driver to stop by the World Trade Center Memorial.

"At this hour?" the guy barked.

"My dime."

The driver muttered under his breath, but took him downtown.

The size and space of the renovations still left Jack breathless.

He hopped out of the cab and moved swiftly across the frozen ground to the buildings and park that had replaced the towers. For weeks after Eliza's death, Jack had come here, studying the long stream of photos provided by friends and loved ones of the 9/11 attack. They remained now only in everyone's agonized memories. He was the one who'd provided the photo of Eliza at her desk, phone in hand. They'd never found her body, so this was where he always came to discuss new business.

"I miss you," he whispered. "Eliza . . . I . . . I don't want to leave you here." In his mind, she stared back at him and smiled. She belonged to the city, and the guilt ate at him. He would have been at the desk beside her had he not crossed the road that fateful morning to pick up some breakfast and collect his drycleaning.

He got the coffee and the bagel, but never made it to the cleaners. He still had the ticket tucked inside his wallet all these years later. He tried to remember what he'd taken to be cleaned and couldn't. All he could recall was the terror and torment of those trapped inside the decimated towers. She would always be with him. And a part of him would stay with her. But he had to live. He had to go.

I have no choice.

Jack returned to the warm cab, which now smelled peculiarly of onions, and he leaned his head against the cold window, and for the first time since Cameron's passing, wept for all he had lost.

At the airport, he fretted over not buying some new clothes. He had nothing he could wear in the tropics. As he waited for his flight to Los Angeles, he Googled Hawaii's temperatures. A pleasant seventy-two degrees. *I'm gonna melt if I go there in these things.* Then he fretted about coffee. *Everyone raves about Kona coffee, but what if I hate the stufff?* He almost bought himself two pound bags of ground coffee at a Starbucks kiosk but good sense kicked in and he checked that the ubiquitos coffee brand had invaded the islands as well. He contented himself with a large flat white coffee and waited for his flight.

He and George took separate flights to California, George being unable to secure a seat on the same plane. They would meet up at the Hawaiian Airlines terminal at LAX and fly to

Honolulu together. On his United Airlines flight, Jack purchased a sandwich that was almost frozen and tasteless, but it staved off the gnawing hunger he'd felt since Cameron's passing. He paged through the file of emails and notes George had put together for him on *Molokai Man*.

Cameron had typed out a brief history of the leprosy settlement, Kalaupapa. He recognized it as his uncle's handiwork because it was full of his proofreading marks Jack had found so hurtful and annoying throughout his life as a writer. Kalaupapa had been created as an isolated settlement for the growing number of leprosy suffers in Hawaii, all sent against their will during the reign of King Kamehameha V in 1866. Located at the base of the tallest sea cliffs in the world, this ancient fishing village had been selected because it was inaccessible to visitors due to its mountainous location, and, therefore, escape proof.

Before Father Damien, the patron saint of AIDS and Hansen's Disease, a Belgian priest, canonized a few years ago, arrived in 1873, it was a lawless place. Leprosy sufferers were denied food, shelter, and medical treatment. Women were raped, and the most depressed patients jumped from the sea cliffs to their deaths.

The disease's origins were traced to a shipload of Chinese immigrants brought to the islands to work sugar crops. With no cure and no resistance, the native islanders were afflicted with the disease. Bounty hunters were paid to notice telltale signs of the illness and arrest sufferers before they could pass on the bacterium.

At one time, almost two thousand patients lived at the settlement, which had been officially closed in 1969 by the United States government when the isolation law was repealed. The government intended to end the settlement entirely, until the late, great Hawaiian singing legend, Don Ho, and others intervened. Now a memorial park and living museum, sixteen patients, all allowed to live there until their deaths, still resided there.

Jack became drowsy, declined the flight attendant's offer of coffee as she pushed her cart past him, and he closed his eyes. He was back in the jungle and his breath caught as a handsome man stood, smiling at him.

It wasn't the original man from his dreams but a new one, in modern clothes and a look of fierce determination in his eyes.

"This is him?" he asked, then shook his head. "I'm not ready. I'm sorry. Just not—"

Seconds later, his mouth was on Jack's. Soft rain with a warm, glorious scent of crushed flowers filled his senses.

"What are you doing to me?" the man murmured against Jack's lips. "Why this? Why now?" They resumed kissing and Jack felt his body turning to liquid.

This is crazy. What is happening to me?

The man kissing him pulled him in tighter and Jack gasped, his body melding to his. Hot and hard, Jack's whole being absorbed the other man's energy as they sank to the ground—

Jack awakened with a jolt as the flight attendant pushed past him in the opposite direction, her cart running over his foot.

"Sorry." She gave him a sheepish grin. "Can I get you anything sir?

This time he asked for coffee.

She gave it to him, and he thanked her, trying to focus on the file again. He couldn't get over that kiss. Or the sensation of being in the tropical rain. It felt so real it surprised him when he touched his arm and it was dry.

He sighed and dipped into his paperwork once more. He discovered a slim volume in with the papers. A pale white and pink cover, *Tales of Molokai: The Voice of Harriet Ne.* Jack turned it over, studying the back, which proclaimed it

Folklore Hawaiiana. *I wonder if Uncle Cameron wanted to work with this woman?*

Jack opened the book to a story called The Owl Daughter. He became enraptured as he sipped his coffee and turned the pages. The writer's style was conversational and Jack imagined sitting on an old porch with Harriet Ne as she told him of magical owls.

He smiled at the last line of the story: *And I myself have seen them.* As he flipped through the book, he realized she said this constantly. Whatever she she described, real or paranormal, she herself, had seen them.

Included in the file were several pages of journal entries. In the corner of each page was a black stamp, COPY. George had attached a yellow post-it note: *Jack, I have no idea where the original journal is.*

Jack was not too worried. He checked the alleged journal entries against those in the published book. They were identical.

I was at school when the tall man in the long coat walked over to me. I was scared. He asked to see my hands. They were covered in scars, but the red welts on my right hand I could not explain. He reached out with a long needle and jabbed the finger next to the pinkie. I was surprised when I saw blood, but felt nothing. He stuck it into me again and I still felt nothing.

"Oh no . . . he has ma'i pake*," I heard my teacher wailing. I knew what that was . . . it was what we called the separating sickness . . .*

Jack roused himself from the young Kalino's tale.

Once he found the original journal, this whole problem could be cleared up, he was convinced.

Cameron had written on another page, *Note: Some patients travel, but all choose to return here, the only home they have known. Kalino Garcia, badly deformed from the ravages of Hansen's*

Disease, refuses to move from his cottage on the peninsula because he says people stare at him.

Underneath this paragraph was a surprising pronouncement.

Kalino Garcia, now eighty-five-years-old, had been born on the island of Oahu to parents who met and married very young. His father, an abusive man, thought the welts on his son's hand might have been from regular beatings. A school official told him differently. The entire family was checked, but only Kalino was forced to make the one-way trip to the settlement Kalaupapa. He had two sisters, who, like their parents, had never shown symptoms of the disease.

He was nine when he made the journey, and Garcia described it in one entry.

They ship us with cattle. We were on the deck and it was hot. So hot. The sea got very rough. Some girls crying. Me, I was sick many times. They put up a canvas, but the girls still cry. I was sick until I passed out. When I woke up, we were near Molokai.

Nine years later, he married a local woman and together they had four children. Neither Garcia's wife or his children contracted Hansen's Disease, but Garcia's marriage crumbled after he refused to move from the cottage he called home.

Cameron explained his personal experiences with the man.

His disease has been under control for fifty years, thanks to sulfone drugs. His family lives close, his ex-wife visits often. He still rides horses from the local dairy, and collects eggs at his son's ranch. He is the most fascinating person I have ever met.

The word 'ever' had been underlined three times in red.

Jack flipped back to a journal entry where Garcia described movie stars John Wayne and James Arness flying on a small jet to Molokai to visit the patients who lined the cliffside to meet them.

Mr. Arness was a gentleman. He knew from our doctors and nurses we'd waited all day for them. He accepted our gifts of flowers and fruit. John Wayne took one look at us, some of us in advanced stages of illness. He turned and ran like a girl to his plane. James Arness was very angry. He went after him. He followed him, and we heard him tell Mr. John Wayne that all of us had more courage than he did. He surprised me though. He came back to us and was very nice. I think he felt ashamed . . .

Over the page was a black and white photo of Kalino Garcia. He was a very handsome man. A mix of Portuguese and Hawaiian, he had a wonderful smile and large brown eyes . . . until your gaze traveled down to his hands, gnarled and twisted like tortured willow branches.

Jack read the emails exchanged between Garcia and his uncle and sensed a camaraderie had been quickly forged. He had dipped into the pages of the diary in New York and found it heartbreaking and evocative. So many basic life freedoms taken for granted by most people, were denied people like Kalino Garcia and his family.

Jack knew the answer to all of his questions lay in meeting Kalino Garcia. Was he senile, as his family claimed?

He was about to open the diary again when his seat companion flicked through the in-flight movie offerings on his personal screen. Jack caught the opening credits of *Ghost Town*. He picked up the in-flight magazine and read the blurb on the movie. How eerie. A man has an accident, and suddenly he's seeing dead people who all want his help contacting their living loved ones.

Jack unwound his iPod earphones and plugged them into the armrest. He gave himself up to the fantasy world of the hereafter, his thoughts traversing constantly to the existence of a real hereafter.

He found George at their Hawaiian Airlines departure gate, sipping a gigantic latte from the coffee bar. Jack took a moment to take in George's ridiculous getup. A safari shorts and jacket set with a camouflage T-shirt underneath.

"You're not really going to the tropics dressed like that." George scoffed at Jack. "Get yourself over to one of the clothing stores and find a T-shirt and some shorts. Now."

Jack did as he suggested, but bought cargo pants instead of shorts. As he threw on his new clothes, he suddenly felt better. He stuffed his winter wear in the shop bags the sales clerk gave him. He wondered about shoes. His black boots were comfy but not island-style by any stretch of the imagination.

It can wait, he told himself. *I'll shop in Honolulu.*

Back at the coffee bar, George rolled his eyes. "I suppose that'll do for now. Get yourself a brew and bring me one of their muffin thingies." He buried his face in a copy of *The Wall Street Journal*.

George and Cameron had traveled more often than Jack had. Maybe that was why he felt so restless. He left his new purchases with George after he brought him his food and wandered past a kiosk selling travel essentials. His toothpaste hadn't been confiscated but when his gaze fell on a toothbrush pack, he bought it because he figured it would always come in handy. He slipped into the men's room and was brushing his teeth when he noticed an older man eyeing him.

The man smiled and inclined his head toward a stall. Jack dropped his head immediately, and took his panic out on his innocent gums, giving them a vicious workout. He had never been a man who indulged in casual sex. He certainly didn't cruise public restrooms. The older man waited a beat and, obviously realizing he wasn't going to get lucky, left Jack in peace.

He and George had to wait over two hours for their flight to Honolulu. Jack noticed the same gentleman going in and out of the restroom each time a man walked in there and re-alized he was airport vice. Nice job, entrapping horny men. Jack was relieved when the ground crew started calling out boarding procedures. As they boarded the plane and caught sight of the flight crew wearing beautiful, thick, vibrant pur-ple orchid leis, both men relaxed.

George was in a good mood, which got better the farther away from Los Angeles they flew. The five and a half hour flight was made very pleasant by the inflight entertainment and free meal, which Jack enjoyed to the last bite. When they touched down on the runway, Jack began to feel hopeful that things would go well with the Garcia family

"Ghastly food," George proclaimed aloud. "I hope we get better now we're here." Ignoring the flight steward's instruc-tions to wait until the plane had made a complete stop, George turned on his cell phone and punched in some num-bers. "Hello? Kevin? Yes, yes, aloha to you, too. We're here. How soon can you meet us?"

Jack caught George's gaze, "Kevin?" he mouthed, but George just shook his head.

They were booked at the Aqua Waikiki Wave Hotel in Wai-kiki, and Jack sat in the back of the taxi that took them to the hotel. Agog at the warmth and the magnificent blue sky with faint streaks of cloud, he marveled at the natural beauty. It was five o'clock in the evening, local time, which meant the evening stretched ahead in lovely ways.

Mercy. He felt a tug in his groin as hot guys strolled the streets in shorts and little else. *I could get into a world of trouble here.* One look at the island guys swarming the street, and Jack wished he had the 'pull' gene and could indulge in random acts of gratuitous lust right then and there. *Oh man, these guys are better than a fantasy.*

He smiled to himself thinking, *I myself have seen them.*

"Who is Kevin?" Jack asked for the third time during the taxi ride, but George would not speak in front of the driver.

The taxi turned off the main drag, Kalakaua Avenue, onto Kuhio, and rolled into an alleyway beside a boisterous restaurant called Da Big Kahuna.

"You'll see. We're meeting him at something called Cheeseburger in Paradise, if you can believe it," George said as they took the stairs up to the lobby. They were going to stay two nights and head to Molokai on Monday. "He insists the food is fabulous."

They rode the elevator to the fourth floor. Their two-bedroom suite was surprisingly elegant and spacious. George took the main room that had two double beds and a gigantic plasma TV. Jack took the private room that also had a double bed, sliding Japanese screen doors, and an open window that looked out onto the noisy development of the property next door.

His heart sank. He'd just left this crap in New York. He couldn't sleep with this racket going on during his brief vacation time. He slammed the window shut. He could only faintly hear the sound of jackhammers and cranes.

The room itself was very nice. He ignored the small flat screen TV atop the bureau. He rarely watched it these days, measuring time spent in front of the idiot box against how many words he could have written during those lost hours. He was his own harsh taskmaster.

He closed his eyes a moment and the kissing man from his lovely, lush daydream was there, waiting for him. He smiled at Jack who jolted awake to the fresh sound of jackhammers outside his window.

Rousing himself, he plugged in his laptop to recharge it. From the far corner of the window, he glimpsed swaying palms, bright blue skies and couldn't wait to explore. He heard George unlock the balcony door and let out a yell. Jack got up and looked. George was appalled, shouting obscenities from the miniscule strip of outdoor space.

"How gruesome! It's Hong Kong meets Venice Beach . . . it gives me a headache." He reeled dramatically from the window, sliding the door shut again. "I forgot when I suggested booking here that they'd demolished the International Marketplace. What they've rebuilt . . . it's a monstrosity."

"We could always move," Jack suggested, but they were here now and he really didn't want to do that.

"No, no." George waved away the suggestion. "We can't keep Kevin waiting."

"So, who is Kevin?" Jack asked again, bordering on exasperation now.

"He's our liaison with the Garcia family. Didn't I tell you?"

"You mentioned something about a publisher—"

"Yes, yes." George was testy. "I want to shower and change. I'll tell you everything on our way."

Jack padded out to the small balcony overlooking Waikiki. It was noisy, but oh, the air was fresh and divine. For Jack, it was a revelation. It had a scent, almost thick with flowers.

For George, it was, "Oh, the horror! Look at all those fat people in shorts!"

Then it was Jack's turn to shower and change into jeans and a T-shirt. He still wore his boots. Tomorrow, he'd buy some shorts and casual shoes.

When he came into the living room, he was stunned to see George in a new getup of a Hawaiian shirt, Bermuda shorts and . . . ankle socks and sandals. He looked like a crass American tourist.

Jack's spirits zigzagged as they walked the few blocks down to the restaurant, Jack trotting to keep up with George's pace. They walked like New Yorkers, straight for their destination, not making eye contact with anybody. Years of being hit up with every con game in the book had taught them the wisdom of this. Jack, whose hormones seemed to have gone into overdrive the second they arrived, wanted to stop and watch the passing men . . . oh he'd never seen so many good-looking, half-naked men in one place. *Ever.*

There were also dozens and dozens of Asian tourists . . . groups of them. Getting on buses, getting off them. He realized many of the gigantic retail stores with familiar names from the mainland were catering to them. Some of the more expensive-looking ones didn't even have signs in English.

"We cross here." George grabbed his arm and yanked him across the street. Jack saw a tall, skinny man in jeans and an Aloha shirt darting into the restaurant, and within seconds, George was introducing them. The manager was in the middle of berating a tearful waitress for not wearing her grass skirt, and George blanched.

"Oh, dearie me, no, this won't do," he said, until he spied a huge pineapple-shaped cup whizzing by on a tray. "What's that?" he asked Kevin.

"You buy a cocktail in that, you'll get unlimited refills," Kevin told him.

"Excellent." George spotted the table he wanted, and Jack and Kevin followed. Kevin recommended the mini burgers, which George popped into his mouth like nuts. He powered through two enormous mai tais, and Jack sipped a soda, anxious to discuss business. Kevin, who wore his hair in what Jack thought was the sixties style of balding pate and long ponytail in back, seemed to be in his mid fifties. He also seemed to be nervous. He kept the conversation light. He and George might have been content talking about the eight-foot fire tower at the International Market Place, which according to Kevin was spectacular at night when lit at sunset with a fire chandelier and a hundred custom-made tiki torches, but Jack was burning with frustration.

"Kevin, I'm sorry, I need to know . . . how are you involved in my uncle's business?"

"*Your* business now," George mumbled, swallowing the

last of his drink and casting around for their waitress.

Kevin smiled at Jack. "I'm not really involved. I met George and Cameron when they first came here a couple of years ago. George and I —" Kevin glanced at George, and Jack had a bad feeling now. "George and I had . . . an arrangement."

"An arrangement?" George's laughter was deep and sincere. "You call it an arrangement?" He shook his head. "Jack is like a son to me. Let me explain."

Oh man, I don't think I want to hear this.

"Your uncle Cameron was fixated on finding an authentic Hawaiian story to publish. So Kevin kept him busy with manuscripts, and I spent my time . . . shopping."

Jack stared at him. "That's it? That was the arrangement?"

"What are you suggesting?" George looked at him strangely. "Wait . . . you think . . ." His hand moved between him and Kevin. "That I . . ." He grinned. "How thrilling! You really think this young lovely could be attracted to me?"

"I'm not gay!" Kevin looked shocked.

"That's right, dearie . . . keep telling yourself that." George winked at Jack.

Kevin shook his head and picked up the check, examining it. "What is it with you and Cameron? You want every man in the world to be gay."

"I think each man is capable of it. Girlie! Yes, you, in that ridiculous pile of green plastic. Is that really supposed to be a grass skirt?"

The waitress just gaped at George. One minute she was being screamed at for not wearing the garment, now she was being insulted for it.

"I want another mai tai," George boomed. "In this wonderful pineapple cup."

The waitress took it and ran off as Jack cut in with more questions.

"Kevin, have you ever seen the original journal?"

There was a slight pause, and Kevin nodded slowly. "I saw

it."

"Oh, thank God. Now we're getting somewhere."

Kevin spread his hands helplessly. "What I saw was an old exercise book . . . black and white cover. The kind a kid uses in school, you know, with lined pages. Every single line in that book was filled."

"Did you read it?"

"Oh, yes. Some of it was haunting."

"Where is it? I mean—"

"That's just the thing. The office Cameron was using . . . it got broken into. A lot of stuff was stolen. Two laptops, the phone system . . . somebody cracked open the wall safe. We didn't think much was stolen, but then the letters started coming from the Garcia family."

"When was the break-in?"

"A few months ago."

"You think they're related?"

Kevin looked doubtful. "Cameron wondered the same thing. Tomorrow, while George shops, I'll take you to the office so you can look around."

"Did you file a police report?"

"Absolutely. George and I reported it to the main Honolulu station on Beretania Street."

Jack absorbed this news, but something felt off to him.

"I want to watch the tiki torch lighting ceremony." George was talking loudly now.

Kevin threw some money down onto the bill plate. "It's on me. Tomorrow we'll talk more."

Jack wanted to talk now, but he had no choice.

He followed a very tipsy George and a tense Kevin out into the dusky evening. A group of men ran by in loincloths and lush green leis and paused at a statue across the road, lighting tiki torches. Jack was mesmerized by the sound of the conch shells being blown, of drums, and the men running down the street. It was like a moment out of time, and he found himself feeling disoriented and dizzy. He was back in the rainforest. He felt George's breath on his face . . . heard his voice calling his name.

The rainforest . . . oh man. He was back inside it, only this time, he couldn't find his way out.

CHAPTER FIVE

A small, red bird with a long, red beak was waiting for him on the branch of a tree. It turned its head and flew . . . its tiny wingspan burning orange against the liquid sunshine slanting through it. The bird soared gently through a light rainstorm, and Jack found himself immersed in the primeval, heady place again. The smells made him dizzy—fruit, trees, air—and there was the first man again, not the modern day one who'd kissed him deeply, stalking toward him. Naked, except for the tiny bit of black fabric at his hips and buttocks, he walked with a confident, predatory gait.

It was the first time Jack had seen him up close. *Oh man . . . he is sexy. Oh . . . he is more than that.* He was like an ancient warrior king. His gleaming black hair fell around his shoulders. He was holding a spear, and he immediately pointed the arrow upward, as if to signify he meant no harm.

"I'm so pleased you could come again. Please . . . don't be frightened." He reached out a hand, but Jack wasn't frightened, only amazed at this world of wonder.

"Am I on Molokai?" he was aware of asking.

"Not yet, my love." This came from the second man in the modern clothing. He looked at Jack with such passion, that all Jack could do was stare at him.

The first man put an arm between them. "Not yet."

Jack stared at the modern man, the most handsome, yet quietly powerful man he'd ever met. "Who are you?" he asked.

The modern man was almost on him now, and Jack felt the

sweat trickling down his neck.

"Jack!" a voice was calling him from someplace else. From a thousand lifetimes ago.

Alaka'i. It was a whisper on the wind.

"Jack! Jack!" George was standing over him, hysterical. Jack realized he was lying flat on his back, staring up at a sky full of stars. Strangers stared down at him.

"He's okay . . . he's awake . . . give him room." It was Kevin who hoisted him to his feet.

"What happened?" George asked. "One minute we were standing there, the next you're lying on the ground, smiling. Nothing, but *nothing* would bring you out of it . . . and you weren't even drinking!"

Jack couldn't even begin to describe his experience. He allowed Kevin to steer them over to a Starbucks, and they joined the long line to order coffee.

Jack took in the homeless people lining the sidewalk selling their possessions. He had no idea such poverty existed here.

George tapped him on the shoulder, looking worried. "You asked us if you were on Molokai."

"I did?"

"Yes." George gave him a peculiar look. "You did."

He couldn't respond to this, couldn't tell George that he, too, was having the strange dreams Cameron had been having. He turned to Kevin, his neck feeling stiff. His whole body ached. It must have been from his fall.

Jack rubbed his neck. "Kevin, please tell me something of Molokai. I am so curious."

"What can I tell you?" He shrugged. "I spent time there as a kid. It's remained very much unchanged over the years. There are only two hotels on the island—"

"I told him that," George said. "Far too Robinson Crusoe for me, darling."

Kevin looked pained as he said, "We fight hard to preserve the way of life and the culture." He shot George a look that seemed to say, "You will never understand." He glanced at Jack. "There's a reason we islanders call it The Last Hawaiian Place, because it really is."

Jack said, "I can hardly wait to see it."

Kevin beamed then. "Cameron loved the simplicity and the remoteness. He bought the house from a family he met through an eBay transaction if you can believe that."

Jack laughed. "He did?" His head was pounding and he wished he could lie down, but he wanted to know more.

"It's unlikely there will ever be another hotel, or even a shopping mall, on Molokai, in spite of many developers' attempts to build there. It's quiet. The animal life is simply amazing . . .. Oh, and there are no traffic lights, no jail, no movie theaters, no malls." Kevin smiled again. "There isn't a single elevator on the island."

"No jail? You mean there's no crime?" Jack couldn't hide his incredulity.

"I didn't say that. The island has crime. Mostly drug-related. Crystal meth and heroin are big problems here."

"Just like the mainland," Jack murmured.

Kevin nodded. "Right. Hawaii is a microcosm of whatever happens on the mainland. Whatever is there winds up here. And we get a few freaks and weirdos to be honest, who go to places like Molokai to fall off the grid. Maui gets its fair share too, unfortunately."

"So what happens when a crime is committed on Molokai?" Jack asked.

"The island has a police force. A small one, but it's there. They arrest the offender and escort him, or her, to Maui, which has official jurisdiction over Molokai, by boat."

Jack didn't know what to say. He was trying to imagine being on an island without traffic lights. Without major crime.

They broke off the conversation to place their drink orders. This time George treated, flirting shamelessly with the barista, a young man who looked a little shell-shocked. George always had to go there. It had to be the booze.

The barista on the cappuccino machine swiftly produced their coffees, and the three men retreated to a table by the side door. Jack became mesmerized by the drop-dead gorgeous view of Diamond Head, the beautiful, jagged mountain outside the window. Jack felt a frisson of joy to be so close to such an iconic landmark.

Kevin followed his gaze. "Ah. You love it, too. Do you know how Diamond Head got its name?"

"It was from early explorers wasn't it?" Jack glimpsed the glint of stone in the rock formation. "They thought they'd found diamonds but they turned out to be calcite crystals."

"That's right." Kevin looked impressed. "You know something of our island."

"No, not really. I read that in a magazine on the flight over here."

George laughed. "That's my boy, honest as the day is long." He looked over his shoulder at Diamond Head. "I wish I could have been here in the fifties, when the cool night clubs were here. That must have been something."

Kevin flinched. "Yes and no. It was beautiful, according to my parents, but the post-war years weren't easy."

"I suppose not." George looked bored. "Excuse me. I must make a call." He rose from his seat and left Jack and Kevin to talk.

Kevin stared into the foam of his cappuccino. "I hope you like Molokai more than George. The two times Cameron took him, he hated it."

"Why?" Jack asked. "It sounds wonderful."

"It is. It's beautiful and heartbreaking because it can be very confronting."

"I can see that," Jack said. He indicated the people around them. "Look at the people close to us here. Several of them are on cell phones. Many of them are texting. They're doing all of this while sitting in a beautiful place. Nobody knows how to just *be* anymore. Where would some people be without stuff? Without noise? Distractions?"

"Exactly." Kevin nodded. "If you are not comfortable with yourself, Molokai is a very lonely, isolated place to be." Jack liked the way he pronounced it. *Molo-ky-ee.*

Jack was still trying to imagine a place with no noise. *Alaka'i.*

He almost hit the coffee shop's ceiling. The voice was like a feather across the planes of his face. He felt such longing . . . such . . . love, that it took a few seconds to rouse himself from his reverie.

George returned, a sour look on his face. Jack guessed the call hadn't gone so well. He stood behind Kevin, who said,

"I'll tell you how that place is." Kevin was off and running now.

George rolled his eyes dramatically, then slumped in his chair like an obstinate schoolboy.

"My daddy took me over there and taught me how to drive."

"Which explains a lot, Kevin," George quipped. "You drive like you own the island."

"You mean I don't?"

The three men laughed, and Kevin resumed his story. "Over the last ten years, several books have been written about Molokai, mostly biographies of Father Damien, and his successor, Brother Dutton. There have been memoirs of former Kalaupapa patients. Even one of the nurses wrote a book. Harriet Ne, an astonishing researcher and writer of Hawaiian history, published a couple of books about Molokai legends."

"What was that name again?" Jack asked and scribbled it in his notebook.

"She was a wonderful woman, a local . . . she took her stories very seriously, not to mention her research. Even she, a revered island author, ran afoul of ancestral families of a couple of her subjects." He shrugged. "These are local island myths we are talking about, and she was very reverential of her subjects, so the criticism was quite surprising."

Jack mused on the subject. "They're very sensitive, obviously. I can imagine Uncle Cameron might have ruffled a few feathers being a complete outsider."

"Sensitive, maybe." Kevin raised an eyebrow. "The general feeling I find with many of the old families on the island is seething anger."

"Wow. So, they think their stories are being what, appropriated by outsiders?" Jack asked.

Kevin nodded. "You got that right. And when the Garcia family found out Cameron was based in New York, there was a perception that he was cashing in on family secrets."

Jack nodded. He was going to have to do some major damage control.

"But your uncle . . ." George shook his head. "He got hold of the Garcia story, and it gripped him like a fungus."

"You sound jealous," Jack said.

"I was. I have never felt that passion for anything . . . except your uncle." George's face crumpled, but he did not dissolve in tears. Jack never failed to feel surprised when things like art, writing or music were the cause of jealousy. He realized now that part of George's devastation was that the man he loved had a passion for things beyond him.

He'd never realized until this day, how much George had resented Cameron's creative world. Jack also sensed now that it had been an unseen, impolite guest in his own relationship with Robert. How sad. From the time he was nine, Jack had had a healthy relationship with fantasy. It fueled his days. It was his pilot light.

"God, you are so like him." George's tone was accusatory. He rose from the table, as though he were annoyed. "Mind if I take a little walk?" He glanced at Jack. "Alone?"

"No, not at all . . . are you sure?"

"Let me join you," Kevin said.

That surprised Jack since the two men seemed at odds one moment, and super chummy the next. That was George for you. A lovely, but moody fellow.

Kevin got to his feet, leaving his coffee half finished. "I'll text you the address to the office," he said to Jack. "I'll meet you there tomorrow at nine a.m."

"Okay, great, thanks." Jack wasn't sure how he felt being left alone, but he was keen to explore a little more of Waikiki. At least he could do it alone without any negative remarks from George.

"See you back at the hotel," George said over his shoulder as he walked away with Kevin. The two men stood very close. Jack stared after them, convinced something was going on, but was equally certain he did not want to know for sure.

A wave of tiredness swept over him. He checked his cell phone. It was seven o'clock local time, which meant midnight in New York City. No wonder he was sleepy.

He finished his coffee and threw the paper cups into the trash bin beside him. People pounced on the table before he'd even moved away from it. He walked outside, wanting to talk, wanting something more than hitting the sheets. Jack crossed the road to the boardwalk and threaded his way through the maze of tourists. People laughed and talked, and he spotted a series of bronze statues tucked into the leafy rockery along the beachfront.

There was a statue of the surfing great, Duke Kahanamoku, draped in leis. Jack was particularly taken by the bronze replica of a boy surfing with a seal. The detail was extraordinary. He loved how well lit the beach was, thanks to the gazillion hotels crammed across the road, and the endless tiki torches lighting the ocean. He studied the stern-looking representation of Prince Jonah Kuhio, one of the last members of the Hawaiian royal family. In spite of the lighting around him, it was too dark to read the plaque dedicated to him.

I'll come back in the morning. Jack pushed on, smiling when he spotted a bronze mermaid dipping seemingly from the sky outside a restaurant. The writer in him began composing a story about how she got that way. Snapshots of the old Hawaii warred, in his mind, with the stores on Luxury Row.

Outside the canoe club, which had been in existence for over a hundred years, and at this location for nearly sixty, were Hawaiian words that translated to *"The wind blows, coconut fronds sway, koali blossoms dance on the plane."* He wished he'd brought his notebook, but took a photo to capture the beautiful words, which, he read, were the opening lines to a traditional male hula.

Jack couldn't get enough of these small glimpses into the way things used to be here. He yearned to experience the real Hawaii. He was staggered by the number of high-end shops and the bustle of people shopping. Did they really come to Hawaii to purchase Gucci handbags?

He stopped at Jimmy Buffet's Margaritaville store but the pounding music hurt his head. As much as he wanted to snap up a couple of the classy-lookingT-shirts and shorts, he suddenly couldn't handle the throng of people and panicked slightly when he got lost. Everybody seemed to be having fun except him. He longed for the peace and the tranquility of his dream forest.

Hurry.

He gasped when he heard the word as clear as if it had been said aloud.

Jack quit fretting. Everybody was friendly enough, and he laughed when he bumped into the waitress from Cheeseburgers in Paradise. She gripped his arm and led him along Kuhio

Avenue, which he realized finally had been named after the prince. He found his way back to the hotel. The waitress hugged him and ran off with her friends. He was grateful that the racket from the club attached to the hotel couldn't be heard inside the hotel itself. He counted the seconds until he got to his room, and, once there, threw his clothes onto a chair by his bed. He took a shower and brushed his teeth. Jack slid into bed in his boxer shorts, leaving the hall light on for George. He knew, as his eyes drifted shut, that the dream man would be there.

Alaka'i.

He was right there . . . a flash of heat, circling Jack like a panther. Then Jack became aware of his own feet . . . he was barefoot, and the ground was spongy and soft. He was wearing black and white shorts. Jack owned nothing like them, so the moment confused him until he realized how happy his feet felt. He looked at the trees . . . giant, wonderful trees, whose limbs and roots climbed all over one another. Jack stepped forward, staring up at the canopied leaves making the ground and air moist and dark.

The red bird was waiting. So was Alaka'i. Jack felt Alaka'i's breath skitter across his face and closed his eyes, hardly breathing, when he was interrupted by a loud burst of noise.

He awakened with a jolt . . . realizing George could not get into the room, judging by his shouting. Jack pushed open the wooden screens across his room, unlocked the front door and hauled George in, before hotel security came looking for them.

"There you are," George screeched. "What are those supposed to be?" He pointed at Jack's black boxer briefs, his laugh an irritating hoot in the otherwise quiet hallway.

"Underpants," Jack muttered as George stumbled forward and fell on the bed immediately in front of him, lay on his back, and laughed. His hysteria turned to sobs and he threw his arm across his eyes. His crying jag abated and was soon replaced by snoring.

Jack quietly stepped forward, removed George's shoes and left him alone to sleep it off, then retreated to his room.

He heard George snoring like a freight train as he lay, miserably, on his own bed, hoping Alaka'i would claim him again, but he didn't. Jack turned over, burying his face in his pillow, and was surprised by the loud sounds of traffic. He had come all the way to paradise and there was still the relentless sound of cars. He tried to convince himself he was listening to the ocean. It didn't work. He was used to the sounds of cars, however. At least, he told himself, as he drifted to sleep, there were no jackhammers and no techno music.

He awoke early in spite of feeling jetlagged and, after changing into fresh clothes, slipped out of the room. George's snoring was almost worse than jackhammers. He went downstairs and crossed through the gaudy alleyway next to the hotel, with its bargain-priced souvenirs, tacky array of jewelry and T-shirts, and walked out onto Kalakaua Avenue. Turning left, he walked away from the expensive boutiques and hotels and lapped up the ocean boardwalk.

Groups of men played chess at several picnic tables, and grooved to the live Hawaiian music provided by a group of ancient-looking musicians strumming ukuleles. He got a kick out of watching them. A little farther along he saw an Italian man carving an elaborate sandcastle with Hawaiian and Italian flags poking out of a turret. Signs in both English and Italian requested donations. *If you enjoy what you see . . .*

Jack dropped a buck in a coconut shell ornamented with orchids and kept walking.

He came across the statues of Duke, and Prince Kuhio. He greeted them both, then walked all the way to Diamond Head, and, on his way back, felt himself starting to unwind.

The statue of the boy and the seal was even more intriguing by day. The boy, lying on a surfboard, looked down into the face of the seal, swimming beside him. The seal looked lovingly up at the boy. A sign read . . .

Makua and Kila, based on a book by Fred Van Dyke. This book embraces all the principles of Aloha and respect for all citizens of the ocean.

Jack's to-read list was getting longer, it seemed.

He arrived back at the hotel to a grumpy, hungover George.

"Where have you been?" he demanded.

"Out for a walk."

"Where?"

The question shocked Jack, who was not used to anybody, let alone George, querying his whereabouts.

Jack told him he'd been down to the beach, and George, who wore his best defense attorney expression, seemed satisfied, finally, with the testimony of his witness.

"Let's eat," he said in a tone that might as well have said, "I have no more questions for this witness." They barely talked during their walk back to Kalakaua Avenue. George seemed to know his way around. At least, he knew where all the restaurants were and Jack got a kick out of a sign saying Don Ho Lane. Over an awkward breakfast of blueberry waffles and strawberry crepes at Eggs 'n' Things, George seemed very depressed. Even the long line of people waiting for tables didn't cheer up his sense of entitlement. He was very, very down.

"Mind if I don't come with you to the office today?" he asked. "I hate going there. Here's the key. And here's a map. I got it from the front desk at the hotel. I know Kevin said he'd text you, but I'd prefer it if you went alone. Get a feel for it. It's yours now. You can decide whether to give up the lease or keep it on."

"Okay, thanks." Jack glanced at the trail of yellow highlight indicating a fairly straight, but long, path. "What are you going to do instead?"

Their eyes met over George's cup of coffee.

"I am going to shop."

Jack knew in that moment that he was lying. George lowered his gaze, as if afraid his secrets would all be revealed. Jack palmed the directions and George waved off his attempts to pick up the check.

"Let's meet in the hotel lobby, say . . . five o'clock. We can have a pre-dinner drink, then get something to eat. Some place fabulous. You have an early flight in the morning."

"You're definitely not coming to Molokai with me?" Jack practiced pronouncing it the way Kevin said it.

"I'll meet you there in a few days." George smiled, a drop of coffee trembling on his top lip. Jack felt a little guilty now for suspecting romantic activity between George and Kevin. "I'm going to shop and wait . . . his ashes should be here by Tuesday. I'll bring them to the island. We'll have a little . . . farewell party."

Jack was taken aback by that statement. George was already focusing on his cell phone, so Jack left him, grabbing a taxi outside the Moana Surfrider on Kalakaua Avenue. He gave the address to the driver, who floored the vehicle as if his ass was on fire.

He was a good-looking island guy with an easy smile and nonstop banter. He took Jack to Cameron's office, which turned out to be in a tiny strip mall on King Street. Difficult to access, since it was a one-way street and they overshot it the first time, it took twenty minutes to circle back through the Waikiki street maze.

It must have all been designed by somebody determined to test the mettle of tourists and residents alike. The bottom two spaces of the building were taken up by a noodle bar and a seafood grill vying for patrons with signs in screaming yellow and red advertising specials on crabs and coconuts. Outside the noodle bar, a harried young Asian mother was having trouble feeding a weepy brood of tiny children from large cartons . . . not a good ad for the noodles.

Jack stared at the half-finished buildings around them. *Holy, moly*. Was the entire city of Waikiki under construction? He was stunned to read a sign proclaiming that the buildings had been demolished to pave the way for the new railway line. It was the first Jack had heard of it and, as he climbed up a weathered, dipping set of stairs, he knew he couldn't imagine keeping the office space here. On the second floor, two offices were vacant. Three were occupied. The immediate one to the right was a notary public who was also peddling exercise equipment and eyebrow threading. Jack actually laughed. What an odd mix of businesses for one person.

He squeezed along the narrow path and found the door to Keystone Press. A sign on the wall beside it, with an embossed starfish above the name, looked expensive. It was incongruous in the otherwise shabby surroundings. The door unlocked with difficulty, but he was surprised when he opened it and detected aftershave. Somebody had recently been in here.

He recognized the scent. *George.*

Jack shook his head. George had been in here. To do what? Jack groped for a light switch. A desk, barren except for a blotter and telephone, stood to his left. To his right was a tall bamboo bookshelf stacked with books. To the right of this were a sofa and a bamboo coffee table. The office walls were painted white. He noticed two holes in the wall facing him, and he reached forward. Spackle came away on his fingertips.

George had removed something from the wall, maybe artwork, and attempted to fill in the holes. Or was it something taken during the robbery he'd mentioned? Jack glanced around the office, surprised that it was so . . . dingy. When he raised the blinds above the sofa, light flooded in, revealing a view of the Honolulu marina, with its yachts and masts bobbing like a moving picture. Now he understood why Cameron had chosen this place.

He opened the desk drawers. Nothing.

This was ridiculous. Could *everything* have been stolen? He found a second office, which was also strangely empty, save for some books on a raised shelf. He sensed that George and Kevin had done more than clean up after the robbery. They had removed anything belonging to Cameron.

Jack put his laptop bag on the desk in the front room and sat in the swivel chair, gazing out at his view. He picked up the phone and was pleased to find a dial tone. He called the Honolulu Police Department on Beretania Street and inquired about the robbery report.

It took almost half an hour to find somebody willing to help him. He was told he'd need to come down in person to view the file. He wasn't taking any chances this time, and walked the mile and a half to the station rather than risk a lengthy cab ride. The station was bustling with drunks, druggies and a homeless woman who came in with more than a dozen cats in cages. She'd been ousted from the street where she lived. The cats looked miserable and cramped, but actually well fed. They peered out at the humans arguing about them, as though hoping they'd get an early release.

Jack showed his identification and sat on a bench to view the report. It listed a host of things removed from the premises. No mention of missing artwork. He noticed the report had been filed by somebody named Rangsan Sullivan. Sullivan was George's last name . . . but who the heck was Rangsan? He or she had had provided an address on the bottom of the form. Jack copied it in his notepad. It appeared to be a private residence, not a hotel. He sat with his thoughts for a minute, then slowly made his way back to the office.

Once inside, he fired up the laptop and sent a silent thanks to the notary public nextdoor for not having a password on his or her server. He was able to get online without a hitch. Jack scoured the Internet for anything and everything written about *Molokai Man*. Despite a couple of glowing reviews from the local papers, the only other article was a piece from the local Molokai paper, *The Dispatch*, which had a small article about the disputed journal . . . very small. It was overshadowed by a census report that most people living in Kawao county were single. One hundred and forty-seven of them floating listless, on an island numbering eight thousand residents. Jack was suddenly filled with longing for this mythical, mysterious place.

Now, he didn't want to wait. He wanted to go there today. He reached into his pocket for the key he already had to the house. Damn. He didn't know the address. He tried George's cell phone then tried the hotel room. He locked up the office and stepped outside, accidentally tripping up the faded doormat. Lying underneath it was an official-looking letter addressed to Cameron.

Jack tore it open. The letter surprised him. Cameron had been contacted three months ago by a Hang Si Li of the city planning committee, regarding a payment Cameron accepted to vacate the office, which was due to be demolished in two months. Cameron's lack of response meant that any further delay would result in a fine, and possible confiscation of Cameron's furnishings. Jack read the letter again. George must have known about this. What the heck was he playing at? And where did the money go? Did George *want* Cameron's publishing firm to be shut down and forced out? The letter was dated a week ago.

Letting himself back inside, Jack looked over the

bookshelves and decided there was nothing he wanted. George appeared to have removed anything of value, which pissed Jack off. He called the phone number on the letter and left a message for Hang Si Li, saying he would make sure the office was vacated by the end of the week. He left his New York cell phone number in case the man wanted to talk to him.

He locked the door again and ran downstairs, where he contemplated calling an Uber, but flagged down a taxi passing by. Jack intended to head to the address listed on the police report and was shocked when he got the same taxi driver.

"We need to stop meeting like this," the driver joked. "People might talk."

Jack smiled and braced himself for the moment the taxi driver took off like a rocket. They headed up toward the mountains, Jack enthralled when they wound their way along a street named Nohea. The temperature had dropped. It was cool and tranquil . . . and the house itself looked expensive.

"Can you wait for me?" he asked the driver.

"For you, anything." He found the driver's gaze on him through the rear view mirror. Man, could this be for real? *The guy is coming on to me.*

He stepped out of the taxi, leaving his laptop on the backseat, as solid proof he was returning. The house, a low-lying, ranch style property, looked deserted. He walked down the steep driveway, taking in the lush landscaping, and peered through the narrow front windows beside the front door. The house was lavishly decorated. A fresh newspaper sat on the doorstep. Somebody had to be living here. He was about to knock, but heard voices.

Jack felt terribly voyeuristic, but he had to know . . . He crept around the side of the house, the voices closer now, thanks to an open window.

" . . . well, why can't he know about me?"

"Look, it's not the right time." *George. Oh man, who is he talking to?*

"You're ashamed of me."

A sigh. "Of course I'm not. I adore you. He'll be gone tomorrow. We can spend all our time together."

"I want you to tell him!"

"We've been through this . . . it's not that easy. He will not understand it. He believes in true love . . . he . . ."

Jack stifled a gasp when he heard the sound of kissing. He dropped down, creeping along farther, and peered through the open window. A naked George was pressed against a very young man. He was Asian, and he, too, was naked, and begging George to make love to him.

Jack was so astonished, he almost hit his head on the open window. He ran for the taxi.

George had a very young man. Cameron must have found out.

"Son?"

Jack stopped in his tracks. *George.* He slowly turned. George was wearing a robe now, and hastily gathering the folds around him.

"Jack, it's not what it looks like."

"Oh . . . please. First Robert and now you?"

"Look, I never meant for you to find out this way."

"Well, I did." Jack looked up the driveway, and was relieved to see the taxi was still waiting for him.

"Wait."

He hadn't given Robert a chance when he had said the exact same thing. Hadn't wanted to release the crazy, hurt kid still inside the tough New Yorker. He whirled around. "He found out, didn't he, George?"

"Who?"

"Come on, George. Cameron. That's why he left me everything."

George stared at him, as if weighing his response. "No, Jack. It wasn't like that."

"Oh really?" He couldn't keep the sneer from his voice. "What was it like?"

George hesitated. "He belongs to both of us."

"Belongs to . . ." Jack stared at him, horror skittering across his brain.

"Rangsan is our house boy . . . our . . . you know. Don't look at me like that, Jack. I did it for him!"

But Jack was fast . . . too fast for a naked man in a bathrobe. He bounded up the driveway and reached the cab as George wheezed up behind him.

"He left me this house free and clear."

"Good."

"Don't do this. Come and meet him. Rangsan is very . . . pliant."

Jack opened the rear passenger door and stopped. He stared at George. "How lovely for you. What I want is the address for the house on Molokai."

"Don't leave like this."

"I have to, George. Or else I will beat the hell out of you."

George's expression turned bleak. "It's on Kaluakoi Road in Kaunakakai. I'll text you the name. It's called Makai Hale, The Sea House . . . everybody knows it. It's painted green." He paused. "I'm so sorry. I wanted to bring you here for dinner tonight . . . tell you over cocktails. I thought — "

"No. I don't want to know what you thought. I hate you for this."

Jack climbed into the taxi and slammed the door. He opened it again. "Oh, and by the way, I know about the train line and how Cameron was supposed to vacate the office. I told the city planning office we'd be out by the end of the week. I'll leave it in your capable hands, shall I?" Jack seethed with fury when he saw Rangsan join George wearing a tiny Speedo.

"Do your thing," Jack told the driver, not surprised to see

the meter was at one hundred dollars.

"I live close."

Jack's eyes met the grave brown Polynesian eyes in the rear view mirror. *No.* "Yes," he said. "No. I'm sorry. No." He thought he saw disappointment in the driver's eyes, even when he paid him a handsome tip on top of the charges, once they arrived at the hotel.

"You sure?" the driver asked.

"I'm sure."

Jack shot through to the front desk, where the attentive staff scurried to get him on a flight, but there was nothing until the next morning.

"There's only one commercial carrier that flies to Molokai now since Hawaiian Airlines suspended their services there. You're already booked on the first available flight tomorrow morning," the concierge told him. "I'm sorry, there's nothing else leaving until then."

He swallowed his disappointment and retreated to his room. He wanted so badly to be away from despair, hopelessness and greed.

"He left me this house free and clear," George had said.

Jack realized George was afraid of losing his little piece of sleazy paradise. He was welcome to it.

For the first time, Jack realized he was all alone in the world, that all the people he considered close . . . beyond family . . . were absolute strangers.

He walked the streets of Waikiki until it was late, stopping by Margaritaville one more time, this time purchasing three pairs of shorts, four Polo shirts, two pairs of running shoes, and a couple of pairs of loafers. He tried not to feel total panic at the amount of money he'd just spent even though he knew he needed these things. With a sigh, he returned to his room.

After he packed, showered and cleaned his teeth, he fell into bed. Neither Alaka'i or the modern man invaded his sleep, but he was not really surprised. Somehow, Jack knew the day's events, the seamy side of the life he'd thought he loved, was not conducive to spiritual contact . . . to the majestic man who, for now, was on the other side of the veil.

"I love you," he whispered, on the verge of sleep, startled by the sensation of lips pressed against his. Real or imagined, it was one of the sweetest kisses he had ever been given.

CHAPTER SIX

It seemed like destiny when Jack boarded the Mokulele Airlines nine-seat turboprop plane taking him to Molokai the following morning. The passengers endured a bumpy, scary takeoff until an excited flight attendant announced over the sound system to the twelve people on board that this was the twelfth anniversary of the day Saint Damien of Molokai had been canonized.

Jack was not a religious man, but he'd come to think of Damien as *his* saint already. He longed to visit his grave and take him flowers. He wanted to see the buildings the great priest had built.

"This was a proud day for all Hawaiians since this is our very first saint, and a very, very proud day for our tiny island," the flight attendant said.

There was a burst of applause, and the almost empty half-hour flight meant everyone on board engaged in a lot of excited discussion. In the short time it took to cross the island of Maui and then land at Ho'oleha Airport, Jack was given written instructions to buy bread at Kanemitsu's Bakery.

"If you want the coconut bread, which is the best bread ever, be there as it comes hot out of the oven each night at eleven o'clock. That's our idea of a night life," one elderly gentleman told him. "We line up for bread."

Jack struck a rapport with the engaging octogenarian, Mike, and his wife Linda, who were writers. After they discovered that he, too, was a writer, they promptly invited him to dinner.

His first glimpse of Molokai revealed impossibly green mountains and spectacular, golden valleys dipping down to huge waves. It took his breath away.

Mike leaned over to him. "Makes me think of Kanemitu's honey-dipped fried chicken. Mebbe I have food on the brain." He laughed, but now, Jack was hungry too. He focused on the scenery as the plane swooped down to a landing. Mike went on. "Here's something else for you to chew on. There are no tour buses, no big, ugly hotels, no designer boutiques . . . it's truly the last Hawaiian island."

At the airport, Jack rented a car at Dollar. He was the only person in line, and Mike had been right. There were no tour buses. Since there was no public transportation on the island, he wanted to be able to get around easily. He was grateful he booked ahead of time at LAX, hoping it would expedite things on Molokai. *Talk about wishful thinking.*

"You visiting long?" the kiosk attendant asked.

"Not sure. I may stay a while."

"You work for McAfee?"

That surprised Jack. "The computer people? No."

"What about Monsanto?"

Jack squinted at him. Weren't these the people responsible for mutant seeds? "No. I'm a writer."

The attendant pointed to a brand new Ford Fusion. "You can have that. What kine insurance you got, eh? Up to a million dollars?"

Is this guy kidding? "Ah. No. Not that much. I got isurance through American Express. They said it would give me full coverage. I want to rent for a week then take it from there if I decide to stay longer."

The attendant looked pissed. Jack pulled up the lengthy confirmation code from his emails and handed over his cell phone, relieved that he had WiFi coverage. The attendant pecked away at his computer keys with one stubby finger, a surly expression on his face.

Jack glanced at the silver Ford Fusion, thrown by the sticker in the vehicle's rear window that read, "*Molokai For Visiting Only.*"

At first, he wondered if it meant it was a rental for visitiors only, but he soon realized it was a passive-aggressive rebuke to travelers.

"You staying at a hotel?"

"No. I—"

"AirBnB?"

"No. I have a house here." Jack felt the weight of astonishment from the attendant's sharp gaze.

"What kine house?"

"It was my uncle's house. He left it to me. In Kaunakakai." Jack frvently hoped he'd pronounced it properly. He knew every letter of the Hawaiian alphabet was enunciated in a word.

"Huh. Okay." The attendant paused. "What street in Kaunakakai?"

"Um, Kaluakoi Road. I don't know the number. It's painted green and it's called The Sea House. I can't remember the Hawaiian name, I'm sorry. This is my first time on Molokai."

The attendant scowled at him. "You got a passport?"

"I didn't bring—I gave you my ID. I'm from New York."

"Oh. Yeah. Okay." The attendant scratched his chin for a moment. He seemed reluctant to hand back Jack's driver's license and credit card, but gave them to him, then passed him a key for the vehicle. He reached into a box beside him and took out a colorful local magazine with a map making up the center pages.

He drew a line in a blue pen indicating the way Jack should go. "There are no traffic lights and well, no traffic," the attendant said, finally cracking something resembling a smile. "It's five miles to Kaunakakai. Have fun!"

Jack got in the vehicle, tickled that it had only ten miles on it. Whoever had rented it before obviously hadn't covered the whole island, which he already knew was forty miles long and ten miles wide. It was also only seven miles across the sea to Maui. If the locals got too aggressive, he could always head there for a break.

He took off for the southern end of the island, on the one and only main road. Several times on the short drive he had to pull his attention away from the mesmerizing scenery, to focus on the road.

He arrived in Kaunakakai, taken by the cowboy vibe to the clapboard houses. Many had horses grazing out front, some had boats, kayaks or canoes. Barnyard animals roamed freely. He laughed when he spotted a cat and a peacock sitting side by side on the hood of a car in one driveway.

And then he saw it . . . the sea-green house whose shade complemented the rich canopy of trees surrounding it. The garden was in full bloom, with a proliferation of tropical plants and flowers. It was stunning. Giant brown-red butter-flies flitted around, dazzling him with their mere presence. He couldn't remember the last time he'd seen a butterfly. He felt his shoulders dropping about two inches. He was starting to relax for the first time in years.

"Wow," he said aloud, throwing the car into park. He walked briskly to the front door and, for some absurd reason, felt he should knock. Naturally, there was no answer. He un-locked the door and stepped inside, surprised to find it sparsely furnished. It was decorated with bamboo furniture, but tastefully done.

There were no paintings on the walls, none of the accoutre-ments he associated with Cameron's New York lifestyle. A vase of withered flowers greeted him in the bedroom, which contained only a bed, bedside tables and a closet. He dropped his bags on the bed, took the vase with him, and investigated the rest of the house.

There was a large bathroom, as well as a living room with a sofa, easy chairs and a huge fireplace. In the dining room, an even larger vase of dead flowers greeted him. A line of ants paraded across the wall into the kitchen, which overlooked the backyard.

The kitchen had a coffee maker and toaster on display. He threw open the back door and was impressed to see the garden in such good shape. It, too, had a fantastic array of tropical plants. He stared out into the yard, which was supposedly where Cameron had become fixated with his dreams. Jack felt a shiver of anticipation run through him. The properly had a low-lying fence, and beyond that, miles and miles of green mountains and valleys. It was beautiful and rustic. A porch swing, matching sofa, and a hammock tickled his senses.

I think I'm going to love it here.

Back inside, he found the kitchen cupboards were well-stocked with name brand electrical items, and Pottery Barn dishes and glasses, but the only food items were packets of salt and sugar. Suddenly, he was starving.

He emptied out the vases, happy to find a dishwasher in residence, and suddenly realized there were no books in the house, and not even a desk . . . nothing to indicate Cameron's foray into publishing. If George or Kevin had been here to sanitize the place, they'd done a good job. The house felt good, but it did not feel endemic to Cameron.

I did it for him, George had screamed, about their apparently lusty arrangement with their houseboy. From what he had seen of the house in Honolulu, it was more in keeping with the Cameron he knew.

He paused. Jack remembered now that he owned this house. It was all his. He stood still for a moment and rested his head against the cabinet door. Nothing. *I can't hear a thing.*

Ignoring the ants, the only thing that spoiled his picture-perfect paradise, he left the house again.

His smile grew wider and wider as he drove back toward Ala Malama, the main street he'd passed, wondering briefly if he had cable or internet access in the house. He could use his cell phone, but he'd need a bigger screen at some point since he had to work. He was giddy over no traffic signals, and a few drivers he passed actually waved at him. Jack waved back.

He stopped at the aptly named Friendly Market, which according to Google was an old-fashioned grocery store right here in the neighborhood. According to reviews, it hadn't changed much since the 60s. Jack liked the place There was tons of street parking, and only a smattering of vehicles. There seemed to be either dilapidated local trucks and cars, or shiny new rentals. People wandered from store to store. He loaded up on everything he could think of that he might want to eat or drink, and tossed in firewood, matches, candles, soap, and dishwashing liquid.

He was checking out a package of fresh island fish when he felt a tap on his shoulder.

"Small island." It was Mike and Linda from the plane. "I'd buy that fish if I were you. Fresh fish sells fast here," Mike said. "They'll put it on ice for you."

"Oh, okay thanks." Jack paid for everything and accepted their offer to join them for lunch, stuffing his many bags of food into the trunk of the rental.

At Molokai Pizza, just down the block, he noticed a lot of activity as they took an outside table. The waitress ambled out, and they ordered drinks and the house pizza. The drinks arrived within minutes. The pizza took about half an hour to arrive and turned out to be a pretty good pepperoni. Jack used the time to pepper Mike and Linda with questions about phone, cable TV, and Internet.

"You have a cell phone and the best reception is right here on this street and the highway you took here from the airport.

Contact Hawaiian Telecom," Mike said. "They're pretty good, pretty fast setting up residential service. They can bundle your TV, internet, a landline, which is a must here since cell phone service can be so spotty.

"Until you're all set up, Stanley's Café down the road has a couple of computers and a printer, but like most island businesses, closes shop the second it gets dark. It's a ghost town at sunset," Mike said.

A thrill of . . . something . . . shot through Jack.

Linda sucked the last of her drink through a straw. "How long are you planning to be here, Jack?"

"I don't know, to be honest. I'm here on family business."

"Your family has a business here?" She seemed flabbergasted.

"No. My uncle owns a house. I inherited it . . . came to see what I've gotten myself into." He wasn't sure how much to tell them about *Molokai Man*. He was, however, curious to know, since they were both writers, if they had read it, so he asked. They stared at him in further surprise.

"Sure . . . you mean the Kalino Garcia journal, right?" Linda asked.

"Yes."

"I read it," Mike said. "It seemed authentic . . . well, plausible, anyway. We know the family. They're nice people. I heard they're upset about the book, though. They say they were never paid for it."

Jack gaped at him. "They're not disputing the journal's existence?" Jack was confused now.

Mike shrugged. "I don't know about that. I do know they're griping about money. Loudly. That's all I know."

"My uncle published it," Jack said, and he noticed a chill descend between them.

Their pizza arrived and they swiftly changed topics.

Jack's lunch with Mike and Linda had been strained after he told them Cameron had published the book. He'd paid for the meal, relieved that when he learned the café only accepted cash that he had enough to cover it. Pizza on Molokai wasn't cheap. *These are New York prices!* There was an ATM machine inside the café and Jack was astounded to find that if he needed cash from it, there was a five-dollar service fee.

They'd bantered pleasantly enough, but Jack was betting he wouldn't be getting a dinner invitation anytime soon from Mike and Linda. He returned home, noticing for the first time a driveway with a garage. He got out of his car and opened the garage door. It opened rustily, and an oil spot on the ground indicated a car had been parked there . . . but when?

He went back to his car and retrieved his groceries. Inside the house, he was shocked to see a fresh vase of flowers in the bedroom, right where the original vase had been. He was so stunned he almost dropped the heavy bags in his arms.

Racing to the living room, he saw that vase was also full. Oddly, there were no ants marching along the wall. It was a good thing too. He had forgotten to buy something to deal with them.

"Hello?" he said aloud. Feeling foolish, he left everything in the kitchen and ran around the house. Nothing. He even checked the shower, the closets and under his bed. He could have imagined the dead flowers . . . but he knew he had not. He busied himself putting everything away and then he heard a phone ringing. He was surprised to find an old-fashioned dial phone mounted on the wall. He picked up on the fourth ring.

"Hello, Cameron? Man . . . I was starting to worry about you. Lookit, the car's been ready for weeks. I need to get it out of here."

Jack paused. "I'm his nephew . . . Cameron died a few days ago."

A murmur of condolence on the other end of the phone. Within seconds, Jack had directions and was leaving the house.

He drove to the mechanic's shop, which was twenty miles away in the Halawa Valley on the far southern part of the island. He drank in the lush scenery, easily finding Joe's small mom and pop business two doors down from a macadamia farm as the mechanic had described. Jack turned off the engine and listened. Water . . . he was in the shadow of a great waterfall. He saw it off in the distance as he crossed the tire-strewn front yard of Joe's driveway.

"Hey," Joe said, coming out to greet him. He was a chubby, middle-aged white guy in overalls and, Jack realized when the guy turned sideways, nothing underneath it. "She's over there." Joe indicated with an oily rag, and Jack turned to see a black Ford pickup truck.

"That belonged to Cameron?" Jack was surprised. It was such a . . . macho vehicle for his artistic, sensitive uncle. "What was wrong with it?"

"Beats me. He said it was driving funny. Asked me to give it a thorough checkup . . . nothing wrong with it. I gave her an oil change, but she's been sittin' here about a month, and the wife's been givin' me some drama about it."

Jack was full of surprised admiration. Joe could have made up anything about the vehicle's problems and he would be none the wiser.

"How much do I owe you?"

Joe gave him an apologetic look. "Two hundred and thirty dollars. I have to charge storage fees because I made the wife park on the street."

Jack almost laughed. "Well, I need to find someone to drive it for me. I came in the rental."

"No problem. Lookit . . . the wife and I will come with you. I'll drive the truck and she'll bring me back home."

"I'd like to return the rental, Jack said.

"No problem. She can drive her car. I'll drive the truck and you can beat the hell out of the rental until we return it."

Jack laughed as he opened his wallet and produced a credit card. Joe took it between his pork-like thumb and forefinger.

"Mind if I drive the truck?" he asked Joe.

"Nope. I guess it's yours now, eh? I am sorry about Cameron. I liked him. Not sure what it was about him . . . I met him up at the hotel . . . the wife and I went to listen to music. He was cool. About a month ago, he called me. He was frantic. I checked the truck over. It was fine."

Joe ran the card through an old-fashioned machine that Jack felt was a museum piece, then gave Jack a credit slip to sign and their little caravan proceeded to the airport. Jack dropped the rental car off and waved good-bye to Joe, who got into his car with 'the wife.'

Jack felt a curious sense of independence in driving the pickup.

Again, it was not what he would expect Cameron to drive, but he was learning things about Cameron that constantly amazed him, each and every moment.

Back at the house, he parked in the garage and stared at the truck. Why had Cameron thought there was something wrong with it? He had the peculiar desire to lock the garage door, but shook off the notion. The untrusting city slicker in him was on guard. The truck was safe.

Inside the house, he hunted around for any other phone outlets other than in the kitchen. None. He set up a makeshift office on the dining table and sorted through Cameron's papers. The sooner he found out exactly what Cameron had left him and what George might try to take, the better.

He rifled through the leather folder again, but apart from realizing he needed to get in touch with the Garcia family as soon as possible, there was nothing new to be learned from the scant papers George had given him.

Jack checked his cell phone and found a message from Kevin, saying he would be arriving on Molokai on Wednesday, and their appointment with the Garcia family was at eleven a.m. Jack was determined to meet the family alone, without Kevin's interference or influence, if that was possible.

He found them quickly in the half-inch-thick Molokai telephone directory. He called, but the phone just rang and rang. *Never mind, I'll try again later.*

Jack found himself drawn to the garden and stepped outside. The afternoon was baking to a warm, rosy glow. The garden was lovely. Tranquil and quite secluded from his neighbors' yards, which were each about three-hundred feet away and their homes were set even farther away from him. He sat on one of the chairs on the back lanai, but felt irresistibly drawn to the hammock. He hoped Alaka'i would join him. Instead, he found himself dozing off, eating pepperoni pizza in his mind.

He was awakened by the sound of barking at his fence. He saw that it was three deer, not dogs. Then came laughter. His immediate neighbor to the right was watering his lawn.

"Unusual sound, isn't it? They picked it up from wild dogs that share the mountains with them. You'll only hear that sound on Molokai."

Jack smiled when the neighbor introduced himself as Malu. They exchanged pleasantries, but Jack was anxious to enjoy his solitude. He retreated inside just as the sun started to set. He watched its full immersion into the horizon from the kitchen window.

Somebody had been tending to the exterior of the house. He wondered if it had been Rangsan. If so, he wanted to put an immediate stop to that. He tried the Garcias' number again and poured himself some wine. No answer.

He hung up, looked in the fridge and decided on a piece of

barbecued chicken and some salad. He was hungry in spite of the pizza he'd had earlier. He took his wine and his small meal over to the dining table, and made a list of everything he had to do this week, starting with organizing internet access. Surprisingly, the salad tasted wonderful. The tomatoes, the lettuce . . . everything had a distinct and crisp zing to it. He helped himself to more and found himself reading the file he'd started compiling on Kalino Garcia Sr. and then his gaze drifted to *Molokai Man*.

He picked it up. Starting from page one, he did not stop reading it until he was finished. He yawned and stretched, then decided he'd join the lineup at Kanemitsu Bakery for fresh bread, hot out of the oven.

He drove, not sure of walking around the unlit streets on a strange island late at night. Twice he braked for deer and wild pigs . . . and then he was back on Ala Malama. He noticed a line snaking around the back door of the bakery. He went to join it and found to his astonishment, Mike and Linda in deep discussion with a man who turned and glanced at him.

Jack would have known him anywhere. He was the modern man from his tropical dreams.

CHAPTER SEVEN

There was a moment when he thought the man would run, but Mike laid a hand on his arm.

"We were just talking about you. Jack Christie, meet Kalino Garcia, Jr."

I should have seen the resemblance to his dad in my dream, but I didn't. This guy looks so angry, he'd never kiss me. He's much better looking than his father. Oh, man. He is gorgeous.

Kalino gave Jack a tight smile and shook his hand. He was a good-looking island man, his thick, dark hair long and straight, a little 1970s perhaps, but it was hot, as far as Jack was concerned.

He was wearing different clothes from the dreams Jack had had and he looked like his father in many ways, but he had a tiredness and pain in his gaze that struck Jack in a way that made him want to hug the man.

Whoa. Knock it off, Jack.

He tried not to stare but dang, Kalino was finer than four mofos. Glossy strands of Kalino's hair fell into his huge brown eyes, and he frequently swept them back with his fingers. He looked to be in his thirties. Jack saw no wedding ring on his hand, not that it meant anything.

Typical New Yorker that he was, Jack tumbled straight into direct speech.

"I am so glad to meet you. I've been trying to call you all afternoon."

Kalino Garcia glanced at him. "I was working." He gave him another slight smile. "Well, you found me now."

"What kind of work do you do?" Jack asked. He had no idea Kalino Garcia Jr. in person would be so . . . sexy. *Geez, I've been single too long. Everybody is looking good to me these days. But that dream. How did I dream of somebody I've never even met! I never saw his photo. God. I am falling apart. Does he dream of me?* He mentally shook his head.

"I run a small book store on the island . . . book store, coffee shop." His face took on a distant glaze.

Jack had the notion things were tough for Kalino. He wondered how much business he could be getting in this remote outpost.

Mike cleared his throat. "Jack here is a writer. Small world, huh?" He grinned at Jack. "So you took me up on my suggestion to try the bread?"

"I have developed an appetite for all things local, and I just arrived today. I can't believe the food here tastes so good. Am I going to regret ever trying this bread?"

Mike nodded. "Probably."

Kalino Garcia laughed. "You just arrived today?"

"Yes, we were on the plane together," Mike said. "How are you settling in?"

"I love it. I have barking deer in my backyard."

Kalino laughed again. "You seem thrilled."

"I am. I only hear cars honking and construction crews jackhammering outside my apartment in New York."

Something dark crossed Kalino's face. "How long will you stay?"

"No immediate plans to return." Jack looked into Kalino's eyes. "I can see why my uncle fell in love with this place."

The back door to the bakery opened, unleashing the smell of hot bread. There was a rush for the kitchen.

"Steady, folks," the owner yelled out. "Plenny bread . . . honest!"

"Buy two loaves," Mike advised. "You might eat a whole one before you even get it home."

Jack didn't think so until the warm, sweet, yeasty scent greeted him as a woman ran past him with two thick loaves.

"Geez ... I do believe I'm drooling. Which one do you like?" he asked Kalino.

"I never met a loaf I didn't like," came the response. As they shuffled to the door, Jack found Kalino warming to him. By the time they each had their purchases, Kalino had invited Jack to come to his house for coffee.

"Sure. I'd love to. When?"

"Now. Of course."

He was tired and, in truth, unprepared to do battle, but Jack had a sudden belief in serendipity. *It can't be an accident that we're both here right now.*

Linda declined the offer. "I'm drowning in book edits. I'll drive myself home."

Jack accompanied Kalino and Mike down the street and up a long mountain road. The brisk walk, the fragrant scents of barbecue cooking and chimney smoke permeated the air, even at this late hour, and awakened all of Jack's senses. They came to a small cottage, and smoke came out of the chimney in wisps. It was like something out of an old cowboy movie ... charming, quaint and not quite real.

Inside, it was just as enchanting. He noticed an altar bedecked with leis, family photos and a definite woman's touch.

"My mother is with my father tonight." He hesitated. "I'm the youngest in my family. My mother was in her late forties when she became pregnant with me. My dad was in his fifties. He was living in a cottage near Kalaupapa. I suppose you know that the residents of the colony are allowed to live there in perpetuity."

"Yes." Jack nodded.

Kalino's expression darkened. "My dad loves it there but for the rest of us, Kalaupapa is like extreme deprivation. You can't drive there. It's a long, arduous trek on a very difficult trail. One of my uncles has a small plane and flies my dad here or my mom there whenever they want, but my dad doesn't enjoy leaving the peninsula much. He prefers being there." His voice dropped. "With his family ghosts."

Nobody said anything for a moment.

Kalino went on. "He hasn't been well. She didn't want to leave him," he said, as if reading his mind. "Otherwise, I probably wouldn't have suggested this. She's been very upset by the book and the, uh . . . correspondence."

"What correspondence?"

Kalino gave him an incredulous look. "All the nasty letters your lawyer sent us."

Jack was taken aback. "You mean George?"

Kalino's eyes deadened. "Yeah . . . him."

"I only saw one letter."

"Oh . . . there's more. I've kept everything."

"Good. I want to see it all."

Kalino looked at him wonderingly.

"You live here with your mom?"

"Yes. Since the divorce . . . mine, as well as hers."

"Your parents are divorced?"

"Yes. He's a hard man, my father. He's never been one for too much togetherness. This is her house. I moved in . . . no reason to leave. It's a lonely place, Molokai." He paused. "We do solitude well here. Solitude and drugs. Over the years it's changed. People come here to live off the grid, but they bring their big-city problems with them. Drugs, petty crime." He gestured to the dining table. "Please, take a seat."

He went into the kitchen, and Mike touched Jack's hand. "It's customary in the islands to always bring food when you come into somebody's home. It would be a nice gesture to offer him one of your loaves," he whispered.

"Would you like some tea?" Kalino asked, coming back to them. "I've put water on to boil."

"Sure." Jack handed him both loaves of his bread. "I'd like

you to have these."

A slight bow from Kalino indicated that he accepted the offerings. He left the room again, and soon returned with thick slices of bread, some cream-colored liquid in a bowl and three cups of yellow hibiscus tea.

"What is this?" Jack pointed to the creamy sauce.

"Condensed milk. It's an island delicacy. Try it. Dip your bread in it. You'll love it."

Jack did as he was told, moaning in ecstasy. It was delicious. The three men ate and sipped and finally, after they'd demolished an entire loaf of bread, they sat back.

Kalino reached onto the sideboard behind him and picked up a thick file. "You have a drop of milk right here," he said, pointing to the right corner of his own mouth.

Jack dutifully removed it with his finger. He had the oddest sensation . . . a flash of Kalino licking it off, and he shook his head.

"These are the letters." Kalino handed him the file.

Jack took hold of them and, with mounting horror, read through the dated correspondence. The first messages from Kalino were friendly, inquisitive.

How did you receive this journal? My family knows nothing about it.

"How many brothers and sisters do you have?" Jack asked.

"Four of us. I have three sisters. They live on the mainland."

"Right. I remember reading your parents had four children." Jack kept reading. Cameron apparently had ignored the first couple of letters and emails, and finally there was a one paragraph, terse response via email. The next contact was a heavy-handed cease and desist letter from George.

Kalino responded with an angry email to Cameron, which was copied to George, requesting direct answers to his questions.

"I don't understand this." Jack looked up and found

Kalino's intense gaze on his face. "You were in the right, asking them for information. They just blew you off."

"Yeah, they did." Kalino looked away again.

"My uncle died, and the first I knew of the book was a few days ago. Do you have any idea how he got hold of the journal?"

Kalino shrugged. "You saw the way they handled me. Aggressively and rudely. I have no idea. The book was a complete shock to me and my mom. We had no idea it was coming. My dad's completely senile. He doesn't do anything except listen to the radio and eat when somebody gives him food. We have to hand-feed him." His eyes moistened. "Three times a day. He insists he's not hungry, but he would starve if we didn't intervene."

"I'm so sorry. I can't imagine what that's like," Jack said. "I'm just bewildered, though. You never saw a journal before all this?"

Kalino shook his head. "The weird thing is, my mom says some of the stories are true. Your uncle got them from somewhere."

Jack felt the slightest pressure from Mike against his knee. When he glanced at him, Mike inclined his head toward the wall clock. It was now three a.m.

"I should let you get some rest," Jack reluctantly told Kalino. "Again, I'm very sorry. I know you're working. We'll get to the bottom of this, and one way or another you'll be compensated." He paused. "Is there another number where I can reach you?"

Kalino wrote down his cell phone number on a scratch pad. "Thank you for not blowing me off. You're a lot nicer than George Sullivan said you would be."

"George said I wasn't nice?"

Kalino shrugged. "He left a message saying if I thought he and Cameron were tough, you would be like a tiger in comparison."

"He is full of crap." Jack was furious now. "Look, I have no idea how the book is selling . . . I have no idea about anything. But I promise you full disclosure."

When they shook hands this time, he felt a touch of warmth, and a frisson of expectation . . . of hope . . . reaching from him to Kalino and back again. He wanted to say good-bye, but found himself unable to speak.

Mike offered him a ride back to the bakery, but he wanted to be alone. Jack walked all the way back to his truck, deep in thought, when a bony, mangy-looking dog approached him. Jack's heart went out to the creature that looked longingly at his hands, as if hoping for a morsel of food. At his truck, the dog sat back and watched Jack unlock the door.

"Jump in," he said. "Food."

The dog understood that word and trotted to the car. He looked up at Jack, who realized it didn't have the strength to jump in. He picked up the dog, and it whined in apparent pain. Jack put him on the passenger seat and drove home. When they arrived, the dog jumped out and trotted to the front door and, when Jack unlocked it, ran inside. The dog peed on the living room wall where Jack had first seen the ants.

Jack was so shocked, he didn't know how to react. He'd clean it up later. He had other things to worry about. Jack took a look around. He realized in the hours since he'd been gone, somebody had been here again. Somebody had moved things on the table. Not obvious at first glance, but he could tell. He and the dog went into the kitchen and demolished the rest of the chicken. Between them, they drank a gallon- bottle of water, and the dog seemed to like crab cakes, too.

Jack let him out the back door, but the dog seemed unwilling to leave.

"Okay," he said. The dog's ears went flat and he turned

and ran into the bedroom.

Jack followed him. The dog stood at the foot of the bed and whined. He put his front paws on the bed and looked up at him pleadingly. Jack helped the dog up and watched him curl up on one side of the bed. Jack had the most peculiar feeling that the dog had been here before.

When he lay down beside him, the dog backed against him, snuggling right up to his body. Jack stroked its ears and, for the first time in a long, long while, Jack had the best night's sleep of his life.

Alaka'i wasn't there in his dreams, neither was Kalino, but he felt a brush of leaves and a fresh smell against his face and awakened early in the morning. It wasn't leaves, but the dog greeting him with a facial tongue bath. Jack laughed. They both got out of bed and Jack opened the back door. The dog resisted.

"I won't close it," he said, but the dog still refused to go out until Jack went out, too. Having slept in his clothes, he felt a little rough, but Jack found himself responding to the morning sun.

"Hey, he came back!"

Jack's head swiveled in the direction of his neighbor, Malu, who was once again watering his lawn. *Doesn't this guy ever do anything else?*

Moving toward him, Jack felt the dog trotting right beside him. "You know this dog?"

"Sure I do. That's Moke, your uncle's dog." His voice dropped. "I saw that Thai guy, whatever his name is . . . he locked him out of the house."

Jack felt his head pounding. "You've seen him around here lately?"

Malu hesitated.

"Please . . . he will never know you told me."

Malu nodded.

"Did you see him here last night?"

Again the hesitation. "They were both here, but it was George who went in. He . . . he . . ."

So George is on the island . . . with his pliant houseboy.

"I heard them arguing. I didn't hear what was being said. George knocked on my door. He asked me if I knew where you were. I didn't of course. He let himself in . . ." He glanced at Moke, who was leaning against Jack now.

"He laughed when the Thai guy turned the hose on Moke and made him leave the house."

"How long ago was that?"

"Three weeks ago. Up until then, Moke was chained up in the backyard. Guess he got tired of feeding him."

"My uncle didn't tie him up, did he?"

"Oh, God no. Cameron loved him. He paid that man to come here and look after him." Malu sucked in a breath. "But sometimes, he didn't come and I fed him. I gave him water. It was heartbreaking, you know?"

Moke was leaning so hard against Jack that heartbreaking didn't come close to how he felt. To him, what George and Rangsan had done to the dog was criminal.

"If you ever see either of them here again, please call the police."

Malu looked at him, his expression fearful. "You sure?"

"I'm very sure." He looked at the dog. "Come on, fella . . . let's get you some breakfast."

A few hours later, Jack had new locks on his front and back doors, and even locks on his windows. He had booked an appointment with the phone company to come out the following Thursday to hook him up with high speed internet, and cable TV as Moke supervised from the sofa.

He contemplated taking the dog to the vet for a checkup,

and decided all he needed was food and water and attention. He had no idea if Moke had a microchip but he'd need a collar and tags. What else, apart from Moke had been removed from the house? Again, he had no clue. Jack didn't think George had taken anything yesterday, and was thankful. As an afterthought he took photos of everything in the house, just in case George planned another surprise visit

He called Kalino's cell phone and felt a pang of anxiety when it rang and rang, but he eventually got voicemail and left a message.

His own cell phone rang a few minutes later. It was George. Jack let it go to voicemail then checked the message a few minutes later.

"Kevin and I will be on island in the morning, looking forward to seeing you."

Jack's body suddenly felt chilled, and he wanted to get out of the house.

"How did you find me, boy?" he asked, and Moke opened up a hazy brown eye and focused on him. Both eyes opened, and the dog leapt down from the sofa. He walked to the back door, and Jack followed him.

He stepped off the lanai and with a whoosh, he was back in paradise, Alakai's beautiful face breaking into a welcoming smile.

Jack stepped forward and was aware that now they weren't alone.

"Uncle Cameron?" He rushed forward. His uncle looked younger and happier than Jack remembered. He wished he could hug him, but each time he stepped forward, his uncle receded, a little out of reach.

Alaka'i stood with Cameron, and the two men beamed at him. Cameron spoke. "I couldn't wait. I am sorry. I wanted to be with him, but I miss you so much."

"I miss you, too. Uncle Cameron . . . did you put the

flowers in the house?"

A tinkle of laughter. "No. That was Alaka'i. I am still unable to travel beyond the garden. But I am always here."

"What about the ants?"

Uncle Cameron laughed, and it was the sound of a running brook. "Alaka'i says when I left the earthly plane, I took all the sweetness with me. You must stay here, Jack. You will find your own true love here. You've brought the sweetness back again."

The dog could no longer stand being ignored and ran forward.

"Moke!"

Jack watched as the dog ran to his master. Cameron greeted the yelping dog with hugs and kisses. He finally looked up at his nephew.

"You found the journal."

Jack gaped at him. "No . . . I didn't."

"Open all the doors," he said.

Jack wanted to ask more questions, but his uncle was fading right before his eyes.

"Don't leave me," he shouted.

"I am always here," Cameron said again, and, suddenly, Jack was back on the lanai, lying on the ground weeping, the dog licking his face.

Open all the doors, Cameron had said.

He got up from the ground and went through the house.

Suddenly, he knew where it was. He ran outside, the dog at his heels. He opened the truck's doors. He checked both. Nothing was there. He was about to close the driver's door when the dog pawed at it. Jack bent down and noticed a screw was different from the others. A little larger and shinier. Several minutes later, he had the panel off, and there was a manila envelope. Inside it was the journal. Black and white, exactly as Kevin had said.

There was a series of papers ... emails between Kalino Garcia Sr. and Cameron. Cameron had come to Molokai thinking he would find a story. He'd found a lot more. Judging by the emails he read, the elder Garcia enjoyed making his family think he was senile. It gave him leverage. It gave him revenge for the divorce he'd never wanted in the first place.

So why had he denied giving Cameron the journal? Jack suspected he was now getting the attention he'd so long been denied. *Oh boy, his ex-wife is going to blow a fuse when she finds out.*

A copy of a check for ten thousand dollars fluttered to his feet. The memo on it read, Advance Against Royalties. Jack was certain the book had sold nothing close to it, and would prove it, as soon as he could get online and investigate Cameron's business accounts. Jack wondered how Kalino Garcia Jr. would react when he saw all this.

None of it explained why George and Rangsan were rummaging through the house and the Honolulu office. Jack no longer believed there had been a real robbery, but he had no idea why George would do these things. And then ... suddenly, he knew.

Cameron had fallen in a kind of pure love with Alaka'i. Somehow, they had found each other across the spiritual plane. George had found a physical thing with Rangsan, and Cameron felt cheated ... hurt ... enough that he hid all the important documents regarding *Molokai Man* from George, who evidently turned over the office looking for them. Things must have been bad between George and Cameron at the end, and Cameron changed his will, the ultimate *fuck you.*

Jack had no desire to take on George legally. George could keep the house in Honolulu, and he could stay in the New York apartment, as per Cameron's will. Jack couldn't wait until the day he could sell his own apartment in New York and use the money to create a writer's scholarship.

Jack did what he felt instinctively he had to do. He called

Kalino Garcia Jr., and found the number ringing and ringing once again. There was nothing for it in his mind but to go to Kalino. He Googled bookstore coffee shops on Molokai. There was only one. It was called Molokai Mule Café and it was on Mohala Street.

It wasn't far, and Jack figured he could use a good walk. "Come on guy," he said to Moke, but Moke ran inside as though a rattlesnake had bitten him. Clearly, he didn't want to go anywhere.

"Okey dokey." Jack made sure Moke had a bowl of fresh water. He'd buy him some dog food, and, he realized that would mean he'd need to drive. He stashed the book papers into his messenger bag and headed to the café.

He felt ridiculously happy at the idea of seeing Kalino again. Outside the long, flat, beige-colored stucco building, Jack paused before turning off the engine. The Garcia family had some class, in spite of their anger toward Cameron. They hadn't blasted their greivances on social media or hired some cutthroat attorney.

There's a reason they call this the last Hawaiian island, he reminded himself.

When he stepped inside the bustling café, he was struck by the sign on the wall that read, "What Happens on Moloka'i, Everybody Already Knows!"

That's good to know. I must watch my table manners, even though the sandwich offerings look damned amazing.

He spotted Kalino who stood at the counter whipping up frothy green drinks for a couple with one hand and taking a phone order with the other. Jack waited, chatting with a woman who urged him to try the kale and avocado smoothie.

Eeew! That sounded gross, not that he said so.

Within a minute, the couple with the green drinks floated out the door and Kalino slid Jack one as well.

"You gotta try our lilikoi cream cheese pretzel." He gave Jack a stern look. "And our drinks are not gross."

Jack gaped at him. *Holy moly. Can he read my mind?* Then he remembered the man had walked right out of his dreams and into his life. *I was just imagining it.*

Kalino busied himself turning out orders as Jack took a small table and ate his pretzel. It was so thick and huge it required a knife and fork. Loaded with warm cream cheese, drizzled with icing that tasted tropical and tangy and dusted with cinammon, Jack thought it was the most divine thing he'd ever tasted in his life. He could have eaten six of them. He scraped his fork along the paper-lined container and knew if he was alone he would have licked it. He figured he balanced all that sugary goodness with the healthy green drink. It was surprisingly delicious. Avocado turned out to be sweet. Who knew?

For the first time since he'd arrived, he thought about his ex. Didn't even give him a name. Just a casual thought. *I don't miss him for a moment.*

People rushed in and out grabbing drinks. Jack thought the prices were hefty but realized they were on an island. A remote one. Kalino's coffee, from what Jack could tell was deemed the best on the island.

"Only place you can get a decent espresso," a pretty blonde told Jack. She told everyone in the café that she and her husband wrote a travel blog. "I'm urging all my readers to put Molokai on their bucket list," she said. The man standing beside her looked a little embarrassed about all the attention.

"Don't," one guy hunched over a gigantic laptop grumped. "Just go home."

"Terry!" Kalino urged from behind the counter. "Be nice."

"I'll be nice when she stops sending other tourists here." Terry picked up his coffee cup, but it was empty. He glared at the blonde as though it were her fault.

"We love it here," the blonde's companion said. "We really do."

Kalino brought Terry a fresh cup of coffee and shot Jack a fleeting smile. Jack relaxed a little. He had an idea Terry might be okay, just very protective of his island home. The blonde seemed wholly unaware that she'd pissed off the guy.

"My husband and I were going to take the mule ride down to Kalaupapa," she said to nobody in particular. "We didn't know the trail washed away in a storm last year and the rides have been suspended. Anybody know when they'll start up again?"

She stood in the center of the café swiveling her head from left to right. Nobody responded. She caught Jack's gaze.

"Sorry." He shrugged. "I'm new here myself."

"Awesome," Terry mumbled and hammered away at his laptop.

"That means we'll have to take a plane there. And I hate flying. My husband and I came here by boat from Maui." The blonde still waited for more interaction. None came. It was the first real moment of discomfort Jack had experienced here.

Jack longed to say, "Is that really the only way to get there?" but worried that Terry might physically assault him. Steam almost poured out of Terry's ears as he glared at the woman.

"You don't need to go there," he said.

"But of course I do. My great aunt was a nurse who serviced Kalaupapa in the nineteen fifties."

Terry gaped at her.

"What was her name?" Kalino asked, coming around to her.

The blonde thrust a yellowed newspaper clipping into Kalino's hands. He seemed excited as he rushed away again, disappearing into the back of the café.

Other newcomers entered, checked out the goods on display and one guy came in with a basket of fresh tomatoes that were so fragrant, Jack could smell them from his perch. Kalino came back out, took custody of the tomatoes and plunked them on one of the countertops. He juggled two books under his arm and placed them on Terry's table. Hunting through them, he found what he was looking for.

"Your auntie's listed here. Annie Davis gave service to Kalaupapa from nineteen forty-seven to nineteen fifty-five. I would be proud to arrange transportation for you," he told the blonde, handing her back her clipping.

"You can do that? I was named after her, you know."

"Sure, I can do it. It may take a day, day and a half. How long will you be here?"

"Three more days." The blonde beamed.

Jack longed to join the excursion and said, "Can I come along too? I'm happy to pay the airfare."

"Done." Kalino looked pleased. "Now, Terry, apologize to Annie here. She's family."

"Sorry." Terry didn't look it, but as he shifted his gaze from the blonde to his laptop again, his mood didn't seem so dark.

Annie and her husband exchanged phone numbers with Kalino then took off with their drinks. The café settled down again and Jack moved around, admiring the collection of mule-themed items. Pre-packaged snacks, tea, coffee, soap, incense, candles, ec-friendly shopping totes, purses, water-proof wallets with the café's logo on them, scarves, hats, and mini mule statues vied for room in the warm, eccentric space. It seemed apt considering the business name, plus Jack knew the old leper colony of Kalaupapa conducted tours on the backs of mules. Well, they would resume again, once the trails were repaired.

I really hope we can go and visit.

He studied the books Kalino was selling. There were several copies of different Hawaiian-based titles. Several seemed to be text books, or at least non-fiction. *Dismembering Lahui: A History of the Hawaiian Nation to 1887* appeared to be popular. There were both new and old copies, plus one marked, *loaner.*

There were also a few battered copies of Harriet Ne's stories.

"You should read that one," Kalino said, coming over to him.

"I started to, on the plane. I enjoyed the stories. I myself have seen them."

Kalino laughed. "I myself have seen them too." He moved back to the counter and returned with a biscuit sandwich that smelled so good, Jack took the half that Kalino proffered him.

A guy wearing a baseball cap with the words *Got Poi?* emblazoned on it, took over at the counter.

"Thanks, if it's okay, I'll buy a copy of *Dismembering Lahui*," Jack said. "I'll add it to my bill."

Kalino gave him a dazzling smile. "The pretzel and drink are on the house. But you can pay for the book. So, what did you think of the kale and avocado?"

"Delicious." Jack followed Kalino back to the small corner table where he'd been sitting before and they sat across from each other. "How did you know I was thinking it sounded gross?"

Another big grin. Kalino looked at him. Man, he was gorgeous. "You had that look the uninitated get when they hear the word kale." He leaned closer to Jack. "Can you come back in an hour or so? We can talk in my office, which is at the back of the café."

"Sure." Jack wanted to tell him now that he'd found the envelope but realized they had no privacy. Hunting around for some excuse to keep Kalino at the table, Jack said, "So you recommend this book."

Kalino ducked his head in a bashful way that Jack found beguiling.

He spotted a woman holding a couple of tomatoes and a bag of coffee. Kalino moved back to the counter, bagged the goods for her and took a cash payment. A few more customers came in. The discussions about everyday life on the island made Jack think of the old TV series *Greenacres*. Minus the Cannonball railway line and an expressive pig named Arnold.

Kalino returned. "Sorry about that."

"No problem." Jack paused. "Business is business. And I do need to talk to you."

"Okay. Like I said, meet me here later." He frowned. "You know what? There's a lantern ceremony at sunset. You should come to it. Meet me here at five and we'll go over together. After that, we can talk."

"I can do that. What's a lantern ceremony?"

Kalino gave him a sad smile. "You'll find out."

"Ah. Cryptic." Jack paid for his book and a couple of tomatoes, then headed back to The Friendly Market and perused the pet food items. He had no idea what Cameron had fed Moke, but stocked up on a few different cans, a surfboard-patterned dog collar and leash, and also bought some chicken breasts, then returned home.

Moke was waiting for him. Jack was certain the dog needed a walk. They both did.

"Come on, guy," he said.

Moke ran to the kitchen door and after locking the place up again, Jack walked with him along the road. The place was so still and so quiet, it was everything Jack had yearned for, but the unexpected nature of it took his breath away.

All he could hear was birdsong, Moke's loping and his own footfall. The dog found everything fascinating. Loud noises startled him, but that didn't surprise him. The dog had been abandoned for weeks. Each time a car backfiring rattled Moke, Jack bent and praised him. "Good boy, Moke. Good boy."

Jack already loved the deep red earth and soon discovered that the unusual plants and shrubs along the path had wonderful scents. No wonder Moke kept burying his face in them.

Jack took photos of many of them with his cell phone, intending to Google them back at the house. It was so strange, yet so liberating to have time on his hands. He was always tearing off someplace in New York.

Would I get bored here? Is there anything to do except just be?

Oddly, he didn't think he'd ever get bored. He smiled at the thought. Boredom had never been in his vocabulary.

After an hour's sojourn he and Moke returned to the house. Moke ran to his water dish and drained it, looking up at Jack expectantly. Jack refilled it, scooping a can of food into a second dish. He had no idea if tap water was okay on the island, but assumed it was. Regardless, Moke seemed to like it.

Jack put the collar he'd bought on Moke. The dog seemed to smile. Jack had a sudden urge to lie in the hammock in the backyard, but worried about George turning up unexpectedly and finding him out there. He didn't want to feel vulnerable, but still, Jack longed for a nap. The outdoor sofa would be fine. If George showed up, so be it.

Moke climbed up with him, squeezing his lanky frame beside him. Jack's heart melted when Moke draped his head and a paw over Jack's chest. He released a deep sigh. Moke seemed content, making Jack feel the same way. Man and dog were asleep within seconds.

Jack awakened sometime later, a little groggy. He had no idea how long he'd been sleeping but it was now a quarter to five.

"Come on," he told Moke, who took his time getting down from the sofa.

Jack leashed him and together, they walked to Kalino's coffee shop. The whole way, Jack wrestled with his feelings. He longed to tell Kalino he'd found the envelope. He would sort out the mess and move on with his life . . . even if it meant no further contact with Kalino.

They arrived a little after five, approaching Kalino's

backdoor. Kalino opened it, Moke parking his butt dutifully at Jack's feet.

"It's so weird . . . I've seen this dog for a couple of weeks," Kalino said. "He wouldn't come near me."

Jack looked at him, wanting him to understand there were mysteries of life nobody could explain.

"He belonged to my uncle Cameron. Listen, this is what I've found."

Kalino held up a hand. "Let's wait." He spotted the file under Jack's arm. "We'll come back. The lantern ceremony is about to start. Let's go."

Jack allowed Kalino to lead him away from the café and they walked down an unmarked path toward the beach.

"It's the thirtieth anniversary of a terrible plane crash here," Kalino said. "Aloha Island Air flight seventeen twelve crashed into the mountains killing all twenty people on board. I had a cousin who was on the flight. A lot of people had somebody on that plane that they loved." His eyes glistened with unshed tears.

"We never forget them and we honor them every year."

"I'm so sorry," Jack said.

"Don't be. I just think it's a nice way for you to honor your uncle too. We send lit paper lanterns across the ocean to help heal the souls that have passed. I bet you haven't even properly acknowledged your uncle's death, have you?"

"Um." Jack was a little taken aback. It was such a personal thing, how one tackled death. Jack had faced a lot of it in his life and tended to look away from it.

Along the shoreline, about thirty people stood, some crying, some smiling. A woman spoke as Jack and Kalino approached.

"I lost my daughter in this crash," she said. "Sometimes in grief, you think if you push it away but in reality, we need to remember their names, remember their faces."

Jack's emotions rose to the surface and tears stung his eyes.

The woman looked at each face in turn. "We need to remember their lives. And how they impacted ours."

Jack spotted the blogger, Annie Davis, and hoped she wasn't going to post about this event. But she too, had dissolved in tears.

One by one, everyone wrote the names of a lost loved one on the side of a paper lantern. Annie Davis wrote *Aunty Annie*.

Jack wrote *Uncle Cameron*.

Tealights were lit and inserted at the base of each lantern, which the participants floated along the water. The colors were pure and soft. Pink, blue, purple. Jack could hardly look at Kalino as they both wept openly. Beside him, Moke let out a keening wail, a heartfelt whine.

He knows. He understands. Jack wrapped his arms around the grieving dog. *How? How does he know?* Moke's warm brown eyes focused on the lanterns. A couple rose in the air and flew down again.

The dog moved between the mourners, who took both courage and comfort from his grief. Jack watched Cameron's lantern as it careened over gentle waves.

I want to come back here again. I want to honor him every year.

There was a moment where Jack thought he would completely lose it when somebody carried a special lantern that he discovered had the name of the twenty plane crash victims written on it. The lantern joined the others.

Finally, the woman who'd addressed them all said, "Everybody had a story. It's important that we share those stories."

And with that, Jack and Kalino traded glances. This was the whole crux of why Jack was here.

His father's story.

And it was also Cameron's, too.

CHAPTER EIGHT

As the sun set, the participants stood in a circle near the shoreline. Gradually, the lanterns left them behind and as stories tumbled out through tears and laughter, they sat. Jack had never met a more humble or inspiring group of people. He heard stories of the gifted young volleyball team members who persihed in the crash, including Kalino's cousin.

"My cousin could immitate Elmer Fudd like nobody could," Kalino remembered. "Our favorite thing on Saturday mornings was watching cartoons and eating Corn Flakes with ice cream." His face shone for a moment. "He wanted to be a singer. He had wonderful long hair. The perfect hair to be a singer." Kalino immitated holding a microphone and flinging his hair back.

Everyone laughed.

"He wanted to be Keola Beamer." His face crumpled and he whispered, "Ah. Good times."

Annie Davis spoke up, from where she was sitting, cross-legged on the sand beside her husband. He held her hand as tears streamed down her face. "My aunty wasn't on the plane. She lived at Kalaupapa, working as a nurse for many years. Her time is long gone. She died many years ago but I like to think her spirit was there when the plane crashed into the mountain.

"She was a nurse who lived to help people. In death, I'm certain she was there." She swatted at her tears with her free hand. "I'm positive she helped all those souls walk the rainbow. I am sorry you all lost such precious people. I wish I could have met them all." Her head fell and many of those around her murmured their thanks. It was a heartfelt moment, words spoken out of sheer love. Jack was certain of that.

Then it was his turn. He'd hardly had a chance to process Cameron's loss, let alone articulate it. He took a deep breath.

"When I was in junior high, I was in boarding school in Connecticut, having a very rough time of it. After I was caned for talking in class, yes I was caned. Six swipes on my left hand. Never felt pain like it. My pinky finger is still broken. It never healed right." He became aware of the stricken faces around him. "Well, one morning, I ran away."

He became lost in his thoughts for a moment. He hadn't thought about the incident in years. "I hopped on a train with no money and walked from Central Station to my uncle's apartment in Manhattan. He was home, and his place smelled good and warm. He asked me what happened and when I told him, he said, "Well, I wouldn't go back if I were you."

The others laughed and Jack felt the warmth flood his system when Kalino leaned in and hugged him.

"I never did go back and my relationship with my uncle got closer. It's only been a few days since I lost him but he loved this place." Jack swallowed. "And I understand why."

When they all eventually stood and exchanged hugs, Jack regretted not reaching out to Cameron more.

Now I think about it, our relationship revolved around food. We were always meeting someplace to eat. Food was our buffer. He loved me, in a distant way, the only way some men can love. Oh Cameron, you old fart. Why did you leave me? Why didn't you let me love you more?

When the group said their goodbyes, Jack watched as Kalino moved away to a small gathering of people clustered away from the others.

One of them was Kalino Garcia, Sr. He stood, balancing himself on a walking stick. Kalino glanced back at Jack, but didn't beckon him over. A few minutes later, he rejoined Jack.

"Let's go," he said.

Jack walked with him, Moke keeping close contact with Jack's right leg. *It's as though he thinks I'll abandon him.* As the shadows in the sky deepened, the warm day turned into a chilly evening. Back at the café, the place was closed, but Kalino made them each a quick coffee and gave Moke a piece of chicken and a bowl of water.

"Okay," Kalino said, when they were alone in his tiny office. "Whatchoo got?"

Jack handed everything over and stroked the dog's head as Kalino read through the letters and notes.

When he looked up, Kalino was crying again. "I often wondered if my dad was faking the memory loss. My mother will take this very badly." He looked at the copied check. "She's gonna be real mad when she sees this."

"What do you suppose he did with the money Cameron gave him?" Jack asked.

"I really don't know." Kalino looked stunned. "My dad has always been secretive." He sat back in his chair. It's always been his failing. And mine. He could never talk about his feelings. His truth. Apparently, he wrote them. That . . . that inability ruined my marriage. I was with a fantastic man—"

"You're gay?" Jack was stunned.

"Yeah. My parents weren't thrilled. Being gay on a small island isn't exactly treated like a fantastic thing. Now that same-sex unions are approved in the islands, it makes life a little easier, but my husband and I . . . I guess neither of us were good communicators."

"Do you miss him?"

"No. Not anymore. He moved back to the mainland. I hear he's happy." He unleashed a smile then. "At least, according to his Facebook posts. And we all know people lie like rugs about their lives on social media. But no. I stopped missing him when he ran off with a friend of mine."

"Oh, wow. I'm sorry."

"Thanks." Kalino's gaze returned to the papers. "I'd like to show my mother all of this. And I think we should drop the lawsuit."

"I'll need that in writing."

"Of course."

"Look, I don't know yet how much money the book has made—"

"Probably not much. It's ranked pretty low on Amazon's sales lists. And as far as I can tell it's not available in any bookstores in the islands." Kalino gazed at him. "Is it available on the mainland?"

"Not that I'm aware of, but I didn't know about the book until a couple of days ago. I will know more about that and also I'll get definite figures once I have access to the company's log-in information on Amazon. I still don't have everything." Jack blew out a breath. "I haven't wanted to push my uncle's former companion, who was also his lawyer, but I will."

"You're talking about George, right?" Kalino rolled his eyes. "He's fun to deal with."

Jack winced. "Yeah. I'm sorry, but he knows more than I do. Not that he's said much. I don't know how well my uncle's company has been doing but I have a feeling that I will need to hire a forensic accountant. I need professional help at this point."

Kalino nodded. "Understood." He paused, and his voice turned thin. "I suppose now you'll leave?"

Is it my imagination or is there disappointment in Kalino's gaze?

"No." Jack smiled, remembering his conversation with his uncle in the jungle between two worlds. "I've been advised to stay. I've no intention of going back to New York."

Kalino stared at him in surprise. "Really?"

Jack nodded.

"Well, if you need a good forensice accountant locally, I know a great guy in Honolulu. His name is Mingo McCloud and he's the only forensic accountant I know of. Talented and a decent man. He helped a friend of mine who was catfished and almost lost everything."

"Thanks. I'll take you up on that." Jack shifted in his seat and reached down to stroke Moke's head again. The dog licked his hand. "I don't have much to go back to in New York. I had a relationship break-up."

Now why in the world did I tell him that?

"Oh, I'm sorry."

Jack looked at him. "He was a bad guy. I stayed too long at the party. Anyway, and then my uncle died. I don't want to seem uncommunicative, but George seems to have ah, appropriated things that didn't belong to him. I propose one way or another that we re-release your father's book and give it a spanky new cover. We can promote it." Jack grimaced. "But I know how you feel about tourists."

Kalino shook his head. "The journal is already out there and didn't do much to incite much activity here. We can discuss this later."

There was so much Jack wanted to say, but none of it seemed suitable. *I'd like to see you again. Could we hang out some-time?* He settled for a handshake instead.

The electric shock that the simple form of contact caused rattled them both, it seemed.

Jack walked out of the office, almost tripping over his dog.

They left Kalino alone with a copy of his father's journal, the check and copies of the emails. They also left him with the truth.

He wondered if he could ever call Kalino and ask him out for coffee, but realized he could not. Kalino would forever be reminded of unpleasant business just hearing Jack's name. And Jack . . . he wanted love, and was not sure that the man he was now thinking about obsessively was open to even a friendship with him.

Jack and Moke walked home and in spite of the lack of street lights, he felt safer here than he ever had in New York. He fed Moke again, made himself a cup of coffee and busied himself with a to-do list. He found an email address for Mingo McCloud, the forensic accountant, and sent him a note. Then he spent some time trying to access his uncle's business Amazon sales accounts with dismal results.

Mingo called him several minutes later and they talked at such length that Jack felt a great deal of comfort afterward.

"My first consultation is free," Mingo told him. "If you have time, let's do it now."

"Awesome." Jack had never used the word before. Why was he being so relaxed now? He explained his situation and Mingo listened.

"I just checked probate court files. You're listed as one of the executors of his estate. The other is a law firm of Edward Diamond. Do you know him?"

Jack was surprised. Edward had been Cameron's lover eons ago. In fact, in a brief moment in time when George and Cameron broke up, Edward and Cameron had resumed their romance.

"I know him. I'll be honest. I adored him. I had no idea he and Uncle Cameron were still friendly. They had a very acrimonious breakup."

"He was appointed executor of the estate about six months ago. If you would like me to, I'll contact him after we talk and get a copy of the will for you. On second thoughts, it'll be late in New York. I can call him first thing in the morning. I'll try and find out what he knows about passwords for the company website and places like Amazon."

"Okay, thanks." Jack's thoughts richocheted in his mind. Six months ago, Cameron had appointed Edward to help him. *He didn't trust George anymore, but stayed with him.* Jack leaned back in his chair for a moment. He'd loved Edward but had gradually accepted that his uncle returned to George and had grown to love him, too.

Why didn't Edward call me when Uncle Cameron died? I haven't called my parents, either. Maybe I should.

"I'll email you a contract now. My initial rate for the work we discussed will be two-hundred-and-fifty dollars," Mingo said. "Anything further can be worked out."

"Great, thanks. I've got a pretty rudimentary setup here. Can you send me one of those contracts that allows for me to sign online?"

"Absolutely. I'm sending over an Echosign form to you right now."

"Thank you." Jack hesitated. "I guess my case must seem complicated and weird. The family dynamics are . . . unusual, I know."

"Not really." Mingo let loose with a delicious laugh. He sounded cute. "Most of my business is helping people with blended families. Yours is actually pretty straight forward. I'll be in touch."

Jack found Mingo's personal Facebook page. As he suspected, he was cute. He was more than that. He was drop-dead handsome. But he had a husband and son. They were drop-dead gorgeous too. Jack found court reports and reviews on Mingo and smiled. The man had an excellent reputation and success rate. *I think I'm in good hands.*

He received the electronic contract, signed it, then Googled Molokai hikes and found Annie Davis's blog. He was intrigued by her post about a trail that had been the favorite of Hawaii's very first female ruler, Queen Ka'ahumanu. He took notes.

Moke and I will find it in the morning. Then I can say, I myself have seen it.

Jack dreamed of stars and silence in a large, deep night sky.

Music. Distant. No. It was a ringtone on his cell. Damn. He awakened at five a.m. and checked his phone. He'd forgotten to remove Robert from his address book and the special music he'd downloaded to signal his calls.

It was *Wherever You Will Go* by The Calling. He'd once felt that way about Robert. Not anymore. Jack fiddled with the phone to block Robert's calls, not even remotely interested in knowing why his ex had made contact at the crack of dawn.

Well, it's not that early in New York.

He got out of bed, which wasn't easy with Moke wrapped around his legs. In the kitchen, he organized dog food for Moke, and coffee for himself. As the ancient coffee maker sputtered into action, Jack regretted now that he'd given all his bread to Kalino. While he waited for his brew, he took a shower.

Jack was towel-drying himself when his phone rang again. It was Kalino.

"Hey," he said.

Kalino laughed. "Hey, yourself. Listen, my mom's making breakfast. They want to meet you. Can you come join us?"

Jack hesitated. "Your dad's here?"

"Oh, yeah. My uncle flew him in last night. He's the one with the plane. He's offered us a ride to Kalaupapa. But more on that later. Are you up for a home-cooked meal?"

"Sure." Jack had to think. "I can't remember the last time I had one."

"Bring the dog," Kalino said. "Bet it's been a long time for him, too. Besides, I can see you two are already joined at the hip. Now, let me tell you where we are. I know you came here with Mike but from your house, it's pretty easy on foot." He gave Jack walking directions. "See you in a few."

Jack set off, his new best friend in tow. He wasn't worried about leaving Moke at home as much as he was nervous knowing George was somewhere nearby by now and likely to break into the house. *I hope that Mingo McCloud calls me back soon. Maybe I need to think about investing in a security system. Maybe I should have brought my papers and laptop with me. In fact, maybe I need to be less of a New Yorker and quit worrying so much. George has taken pretty much everything by now and my laptop is fingertip encrypted.*

He shook off his troubled thoughts as they reached the Garcia house. Once again he was tickled by the image of the cosy cottage. *And, oh. Eggs. The wonderful smell of freshly cooked eggs.*

Jack realized he'd come empty handed, but soon forgot that worrying thought too when a big, floppy-eared hound dog came racing out of the house, bounding toward them. He and Moke greeted each other like long-lost friends and Moke loped after the hound inside the house.

Kalino appeared in the doorway, a huge grin on his face.

"My dog just invited himself in," Jack said. "He has no manners."

"Neither does Pete. But dogs will be dogs." Kalino beckoned him inside. "Hope you brought your appetite."

"I did bring that, but no hostess gift, I'm sorry."

"Eh, you gave me your bread yesterday. That was huge." Kalino paused by the small front room where Kalino Garcia Sr. and his wife stood, looking nervous.

"I'm glad to meet you," Jack said, shaking their hands. Kalino's father was a striking presence in real life. He didn't look as though he had dementia, because he seemed so focused, but looks could be deceiving. His grip was strong.

"I liked your uncle, until I didn't," Mr. Garcia said. "Once he stopped contacting me and got his yackity-yacking lawyers taking over, it was . . . wrong."

"Yes, it was. But I want you to know I loved your book and I am glad my uncle published it."

For a moment, nobody said anything. Jack still wondered what Mr. Garcia had done with his advance money. In the scheme of things, ten grand wasn't huge, but the fact that he hadn't told his wife or son about it was bizarre.

His ex-wife. Maybe he's a man of secrets.

Mr. Garcia's attention wandered, his gaze flickering around the room. He didn't respond to Jack, who wondered if Mr. Garcia even heard him. When the senior Kalino suddenly winked at him, Jack thought at first that he might have imagined it, but knew he hadn't. *What's the old guy up to?*

Mrs. Garcia laid a hand on Jack's arm. "Let's not talk business now. We'll discuss things later." She gave her ex-husband a glance loaded with hidden meaning. Was she angry? Hard to tell. "We'll have breakfast, then I hear you're visiting Kalaupapa today. It's quite a trek, you know."

"I didn't know it was today." *George is supposed to be coming to the island today. I'll text him and find out when he arrives.* Another thought occurred to him. *Where are he and Kevin planning to stay? I don't want them anywhere near Moke. And I don't want them staying with me . . .*

Mrs. Garcia nodded. "Oh, yes. That's why I wanted to make sure you had a good breakfast. I'll pack you all some sandwiches for the day. It's quite an undertaking, but well worth it. The old hospital has quite a lot of *mana* attached to it."

Jack knew *mana* was the Hawaiian word for power, and he was excited to visit the historic settlement.

Kalino brought food to the table set up in a corner of the kitchen that overlooked the backyard. It was impressive. Every last square inch seemed taken up with vegetable gardening."Everything you're about to eat, we grew," Kalino said, the pride in his voice unmistakable. "My dad still owns the dairy near Kalaupapa that produces most of the milk and cheese on the island. Though these days, he's not so hands-on anymore."

"I can still milk a cow, thank you very much." Mr. Garcia stabbed a thick sausage from a platter with his fork. "Welcome to our table, young man." He bent his head and began to eat. He ate like a little kid, his arm around his food as though he was afraid somebody would take it away from him.

Jack loved everything that came his way, including the coffee Mrs. Garcia poured him. Moke lay across the other side of the kitchen, eating his own sausage. He looked as happy as Jack felt. Pete lay beside him, licking the space on the floor where his own sausage must have been.

"This coffee is so good," Jack murmured.

"Home grown," Kalino said. "My cousin's farm. I sell it at the bookstore."

"How's my book selling?" Mr. Garcia asked and suddenly cackled. "I know you don't have it in there. I looked."

"We'll talk about that later," Mrs. Garcia laid a hand on his shoulder. Mr. Garcia put his cheek against it, stroking it. Such a tender moment really touched Jack. They seemed the friendliest couple, romantic even. Why the hell were they divorced?

So many mysteries on Molokai. Maybe somebody would tell him. After all, what happened on Molokai, everybody already knew, right?

There were no awkward silences as they demolished the fantastic meal. Jack enjoyed listening to the local gossip. None of it was about people, unless you counted the fact that so many people on the island lived a natural life around the changing of the seasons. The federal givernment had approved restoral of some wetlands on the south-east side of the islands. An elderly woman's campaign to install swings and a playset in a local park had been approved.

Jack was surprised how much he liked the Hawaiian breakfast of rice and fish. Not to mention the delicious scrambled eggs, thick-buttered toast and homemade sausage.

"We should get going," Kalino muttered as he slurped down another cup of cofffee. "Our plan with Annie and Lee Davis is to fly to Kalaupapa, spend a few hours there, and my uncle will fly us back again. You'll have to change your shoes though. We'll be doing a lot of walking. Loafers won't work."

Jack laughed. "No. I'm sure they won't." He carried his empty dishes to the sink.

Mrs. Garcia shooed him away. "Stop that. You're a guest."

Moke started to pace and with reluctance, Jack said, "I think he needs to go potty."

"No problem," Kalino said. "I'll meet you back at your place in half an hour and we'll go from there. Say, you got a backpack and a good hat?"

"Er, no." Jack wasn't sure what to do with Moke. What had Cameron done with the dog when he wasn't on the island? Malu had told him that the pliant Rangsan used to look after Moke. What had changed? Why had he mistreated him? And how had the poor dog fared on his own, discarded for three weeks?

Kalino found a backpack for him and said, "Keep it as long as you need it."

At the front door, Jack asked Kalino, "Do you know anyone I could pay to walk and feed Moke for me? I don't . . . I can't leave him outside in the yard, or locked in the house. Eventually, I have to build a higher fence, but it won't get done today."

"Don't be ridiculous. You'll leave him here. My mom loves animals and he gets along great with Pete."

"I'll pay her," Jack said.

"Will you stop offering to pay for everything? We're friendly people here, Jack."

"Okay. Are you sure she won't mind?"

Kalino blew out a sigh. "Why don't we ask her?" He headed back to the kitchen, calling out for his mom. "Is it okay if Jack leaves his dog here while we go to Kalaupapa?"

"Of course," she said. "He's such a sweet boy." She frowned for a moment. "Mighty skinny though."

"I'm working on fattening him up," Jack assured her. He worried about leaving the dog in a strange place but Moke didn't even give him a second glance. He flopped at Mrs. Garcia's feet as though he had not a care in the world. *Shameless!*

Jack still wanted to take Moke out, feeling the dog was his responsibility, but realized he'd been outnumbered. Instead, he organized the borrowed backpack, stuffing it with food and bottled water. His cell phone was fully charged.

"You'll need a hat and sunscreen," Kalino said. "You city slicker, you."

"Hey, I resemble that." Jack had no idea where his weird sense of humor had suddenly sprung from, but Kalino laughed.

"I'll come with you. Then we can go pick up our favorite bloggers," Kalino said.

Jack blinked. Kalino's words had just sparked an idea he'd had ever since the lantern ceremony. He wanted to offer Annie Davis a book deal, based on her blog and also her aunt's dedication to the settlement at Kalaupapa.

"You okay?" Kalino asked.

"Yes. I—I checked out Annie's blog and I think I'd like to offer her a publishing deal."

"There are people who might hate you for it. But if you're talking about a memoir about her aunt, I think that would be amazing."

"Exactly what I was thinking. I wish I'd brought a decent camera with me. I want to take good photos of Kalaupapa."

Kalino glanced down at Jack's feet again. "Eh, you can always go back there again. I hope you brought decent hiking boots."

"No. I have running shoes though. "

"Humph. Oh, well, let's hope you don't fall." Kalino tossed some Hawaiian words over his shoulder at his parents, and led the way outside.

"Have fun!" Mr. Garcia shouted. "Give my love to the wind."

Kalino stopped and looked at Jack. "He's still pretending to be crazy, even though we all know he isn't."

"Makes him happy, right?" Jack asked.

"I guess." Kalino didn't seem all that ecstatic but as they walked off down the street, his mood improved. "Sometimes, I just gotta get outta that place, you know?"

Jack did. It was hard going home again. They walked in companionable silence until they reached a fork in the road. One hand-painted sign to the left advertized fresh fruit and flowers for sale. On the right was a sign for an organic farm.

"I do love this island," Jack said. "It's a world away from New York."

"You know I went there once. Scared the life out of me. Just so crazy and busy."

"Really?" The news surprised Jack. "What were you doing there?"

Kalino gave him a small, sad smile. "My ex. He's a musician. He was quite a prolific singer and songwriter and he was invited to perform at a Pacific Islander festival in Times Square. That's when he discovered his fear of performing." He frowned. "He hardly sings at all anymore. Really too bad. He's a music professor at a college in Arizona, but his music was amazing. Oh, well. Not my problem anymore."

They paused outside Jack's house.

"Come in," Jack said. "I won't take long. My uncle left some stuff here and I'm thinking maybe there's a hat. Certainly some sunscreen."

"Annie just texted me," Kalino said, holding up his cell phone. "She has plenty. You just need shoes and a hat."

They didn't get far once they got inside. Jack wasn't sure who started it, but suddenly, Kalino had him pressed up against the wall inside the entrace and was kissing him. Hard.

Jack's eyes widened as his senses careened, taking him, spinning, giddy with joy back to the rainforest.

"Damn," Kalino muttered against Jack's lips. "You *are* the one I've been dreaming about." He pulled away from Jack. "This can't be happening."

"But it is," Jack said. "Big time. I dreamed about you, too."

CHAPTER NINE

"How is it possible?" Jack asked.

"I don't know. Never happened to me before. They call it *Molokai molelo*. A kind of spirit song. An emotional romantic calling. I myself have never heard it." Kalino closed his eyes and opened them again. "It's happened to friends of mine. Jesus, Jack. How can I have that connection with a . . . with a haole?"

Jack shook his head. "No idea. Sorry. But I feel it too." It took everything in him to move away from Kalino. In fact, Jack couldn't quite walk straight. *Wow, if I'm this unglued just kissing the guy, I'm in trouble! I guess it's worse for him. He really doesn't want to have these feelings for me at all. Why do I keep meeting guys who reject me?*

In the bedroom, Jack rifled through the closet that still held his uncle's clothing.

"Wish we could cancel the walk." Kalino surprised him when he wrapped himelf around Jack from behind and nuzzled his neck.

Jack took a deep breath. "Slow down, killer," he joked.

Kalino turned Jack around to face him. "You're right. We shouldn't rush into anything that could fall apart in days, maybe hours, then be stuck on a small island with somebody who hates us."

Talk about mixed signals. Jack composed himself as Kalino moved away from him.

"I could never hate you." Jack's tone came out angry and he hadn't meant it to. He found a camouflage-style brimmed hat. Perfect. It reminded Jack of George's crazy travel outfit and he felt the tension rising in him again. He discovered a patchy dog collar with tags. Moke's name was faint, but the landline number was on one of them. He'd put the tags on Moke the moment he came home.

Jack sent a text message to George. *When do you arrive on Molokai?* He added, *Let me know where you're staying.* There. That covered his basic concerns.

Kalino stared at him as Jack progressed to the bathroom, where he discovered a can of sunscreen in the medicine chest and sprayed it on his face and arms.

Kalino grabbed it and examined the label. "This is okay for today, but you gotta invest in reef-safe sunscreen if you're gonna stay in the islands." He gave Jack a meaningful look. "And I hope you do. But anyway, our reefs are disintegrating because of some ingredient in regular sunscreen. It's mandatory here now."

"I didn't know that, but I'll buy some as soon as I can." He grabbed the sunscreen from Kalino and tossed it in the trash.

They left the house, Jack careful to lock every door and window.

"You seem nervous about something," Kalino remarked as they walked down the street. His tone was light, but Jack sensed that Kalino could read his mind.

"Yeah. George, my uncle's lover, partner . . . lawyer, whatever, he ransacked the publishing company's office in Honolulu, and I know he was in the house here. He and his, I don't know what to call him, but they're the ones who abandoned Moke. I think they were looking for the book. I have it, as you know. Well, you have it now." He swallowed. "And thanks to you, I hired Mingo McCloud to help me."

"Then why do you seem so freaked out?" Kalino put a hand on Jack's shoulder.

"I changed all the locks here but I'm worried about George

hurting Moke."

"Nobody will touch a hair on Moke's head. Or yours. This George guy sounds like a total asshole." Kalino stopped and touched Jack's arm. "I can't believe I never met your uncle even though he was living so close, but mind you, people on Molokai tend to come here for privacy."

"Right. Privacy I don't have yet."

"Yes, you do." Kalino squeezed Jack's shoulder in a reassuring way. "You'll deal with this George guy. Listen, Mingo's husband, Fancois Aumary is a security expert—"

"Security expert! I've been thinking about that. Do you think I need to go that far?"

"Yes, you do," Kalino said again. Changing locks is a good start but Francois can give you an excellent system that's unobtrusive, yet very effective."

"Huh. How do you know so much about that?"

Kalino grimaced. "I had some problems in the shop when I wasn't around. Theft of merchandise, food, cash missing from the float—"

"Oh, my God. That's awful."

"Yeah. Especially when I discovered it was my own staff doing it. Now, you've been in the store. Does it look like it's wired to the gills with cameras and such?"

"No. Not at all."

Kalino dropped his hand and pulled out his cell phone. "Look at this. I can check on my staff whenever I like. I know what's going on in the store at every moment."

"Six cameras, wow! You've even got one by the back door." He glanced at Kalino. "I had no idea there was any crime at all on Molokai."

"Between you and me, I had an aunty helping out on weekends and she took so much food and let people sneak in and let them help themselves to *whatevahs*. It was horrible. I was shocked to discover it was her."

"Did she confess, or apologize?"

"She has no idea I even know. I just told her I no longer needed her. I changed all the locks and got the cameras in. She tried coming inside one night but never tried again. I'm texting Francois with your cell phone number now. We can set up something similar at your house. He's the best. And he's not expensive. But *whatevahs*. We'll deal with it, Jack. I've got your back."

Jack grinned. *We. I like that.* "Thanks." He meant it. It had been a long time since he felt somebody caring this way about him. He tried not to think about his time with Robert, when things were better, happier between them. They were interrupted by a female voice shouting at them.

Annie rushed over to Jack and hugged him as though they were long-lost friends. He hugged her back, then shook her husband's hand.

"We haven't been formally introduced. I'm Lee. I'm the lucky guy she chose to marry."

"You *are* a lucky guy." Jack grinned back at him. They walked to the airport, Jack grateful that he'd changed his shoes. They boarded the tiny plane Kalino's uncle was piloting. He gave Jack and the others a wave from the front, and they all waved back.

"We'll be there in about ten minutes," Kalino said, sitting next to Jack in the tiny aircraft that held seven seats. He was so close their thighs touched, making Jack squirm. He longed to finish what they'd started back at the house. As soon as he thought his however, he began to panic again. *I cannot get involved with somebody I just met!*

Gazing out of the window as they flew, Jack was struck by the extensive damage the landslide had caused on the trail. Even once it was repaired, he had no idea how people or mules managed to navigate the scary, skinny pathway to the leeward side of the island.

The view however, was gorgeous. Molokai was an island

of dramatic cliffs—some of the highest in the world. The emerald green mountains and abundant vegetation was like something out of a travel brochure. It didn't seem real. It was remote, and the cliffs so high, they were forbidding. No wonder the old king had chosen it for the site of the original leper colony. It was hard to reach it and hard to run away from it.

His heart leapt at the sight of the Kalaupapa settlement. Perched in a small valley over the rise of some very tall cliffs, he tried to imagine the terror the very early leprosy victims must have felt as they were dropped in the ocean from boats that had brought them from other islands. They'd been forced to climb the formidable cliffs and to live in a barren valley. There had been no food, no shelter, no medical aid available to them. Some jumped to their deaths once they reached the top rather than face a future of deprivation and lawlessness.

Some survived. Jack swallowed over a lump in his throat. His respect for, and his commitment to the Garcia family, had just increased ten-fold.

The Kalaupapa community was still small. The neighborhood looked like something out of a rural 1950s community, which he realized it was. The manicured streets looked almost desert-like and there was the cemetery near a cluster of small, dilapidated store fronts.

They landed minutes later at the small airport strip on the Kalaupapa peninsula. Nobody spoke. Annie was already crying. Perhaps she, too, felt the desolation and anguish of all those who'd been forced to live here. Before Father Damien came. Before salvation. Before any hope of survival. Jack took her hand as they disembarked the aircraft onto what he already thought of as hallowed ground. In spite of the sheer unspoilt beauty of the scenery, he felt its utter despair. It was as though a thousand spirits stood waiting, watching for them, their long-silent voices whispering, *"Do not forget us."*

"I feel his presence," Annie said. "I feel Father Damien."

"I do too," Jack said. And he did. He felt the great saint's benevolent spirit still watching over the place he built and still stood. It was a testament to his carpentry and masonry skills.

"We need to take the bus," Kalino said, "but it will be right on time." He checked his cell phone. "Three minutes from now. It's ancient, but it works."

Another plane landed at the airstrip and Kalino pointed past Jack.

True to his word, the rickety old blue bus arrived. Stenciled on the side in faded lettering were the words *Damien Tours*.

Jack's cell phone buzzed. He had a text message from Francois Aumary.

Hey there! Got Kalino's message. You probably know I'm Mingo's husband. He wants to talk to you urgently and we're available tonight. We can be on Molokai at 6 pm. We can come to you. Does that work?

Jack texted back: *See you then!*

He glanced up to see a few hardy hikers wearing yellow wristbands marked with the word *hiker*. He checked his other text messages. Not a word from George.

How strange.

Jack focused on the present. The six passengers from the other plane also stood in line. The mood was buoyant as everyone climbed on the bus. Everybody had their own reasons for coming here. Their tour guide, who stood by the driver as the bus lumbered toward the settlement, was a sweet guy who seemed so wacky Jack had to force himself not to laugh.

"People say this was the site of the lost city of Atlantis," the guide said.

"What people?" Kalino muttered.

Jack's thoughts flew to a summer trip he'd taken with Robert to Greece. They'd traveled to Mykonos and Santorini. People there thought Santorini was the site of Atlantis. With its spectacular underwater volcanoes and bright, energizing spirit, he'd been convinced that island could have been the lost city of legend. He wasn't sure yet about Molokai. *I guess everyone wants to think they're part of mystical history.*

The guide went on and on about the early Hawaiians being blond and blue-eyed. *What?*

Kalino, who was sitting beside Jack, ran a hand over his face.

The mood in the bus plummeted as people exchanged frustrated glances.

"What's he been smokin'?" Kalino whispered, seemingly to himself.

"Wacky tobaccy," somebody whispered back, making everyone laugh.

Finally, they arrived and the guide quit rhapsodising about his conspiracy theories. He warned everyone that there was no food available at the park, but drinks were available at a nearby store.

"Don't leave trash anywhere except in the bins," he said.

They passed a dilapidated-looking place called Fuesaina's Bar, but it was closed.

Jack didn't care. He was still full from breakfast and Kalino's mom had made sure that he and Kalino had all the food and drink they needed.

"Don't take anything except photos," the guide warned. "And leave nothing except your footprints. Oh, and please give us a good Yelp review!"

Jack learned the tour would take four hours on foot. Even though Kalino's family had lived here at one time, he couldn't walk around unattended either. The heat of the day suddenly shifted to misty rain and walking through the settlement was like stepping back in time.

Jack felt as though he'd shifted—for real—right into his rainforest dream. The hospital where so many leprosy victims had lived and suffered, was an eerie experience. The visitors' section was especially difficult to view. A working nurse for the few remaining residents, showed them around. She knew

Kalino and greet him with a hug. Jack became absorbed with the hospital's history.

Visitors and patients had been separated by thick screens and windows to prevent the spreading of the debilitating illness. No wonder early diarists called it The Separating Sickness.

There were photos, most of them old, of the early settlers. Jack wished they'd upgraded the place but also understood why they didn't. There were two weathered, framed letters, sent by the state of Hawaii to two early victims of the ravaging disease dated November, 1930. The words were painful to read: At the top, one message stated, *You Will Be Sent to Kalaupapa*. Another recipient was told:

"You are advised that at a regular meeting of the board of health it was voted that you will be transferred to the leprosarim . . ."

Jack was fascinated by the eclectic objects he discovered in the tiny museum such as forks and spoons that had been shaped and bent to accommodate hands affected by the disease. Old shoes on display had been held together with fabric strips rather than shoelaces. The smallest details of daily life most people took for granted had to be altered for those living here. Jack studied the photos of Father Damien, as he was still called apparently, even though he'd achieved sainthood. Jack studied the photos of early patients, his gaze falling on one strapping fellow, who, now that he realized it, looked like Alaka'i.

"What are you so focused on?" Kalino asked, his voice delicious gravel in Jack's ear.

"This man." Jack pointed.

"Wow. You know how to pick 'em. He was handsome, huh? That was my great uncle. He was sent here as a young man. I never met him. They said he was a medicine man, you know, a kahuna. He had great healing powers but got sick healing people from leprosy. One day, he noticed his little finger was crooked. As you no doubt know, the extremeties were affected first. He hoped and prayed he wasn't sick himself, but he was."

Kalino gestured. "Just like Father Damien. They brought him here."

"What was his name?" Jack asked, his words sounding breathless even to his own ears.

"Alaka'i." Kalino nudged him. "Let's go."

Jack's thoughts raced as he walked with his little group until Kalino turned to them, separating them from the rest of the group.

"There's a trail," he said, his voice low. "I think you'll like it."

Jack, Annie, and Lee followed him along the winding path that held vegetation Jack had never seen before. The colors of each flower were so intense it almost hurt Jack's eyes. They covered a two-mile stretch of the trail before settling at an overlook that gave a breathtaking view of the sea. "We're lucky," Annie said. "We know we can leave if we want to."

Nobody said anything for a moment.

"Do you think your aunt wanted to leave?" Jack asked her.

Annie gave him a sweet, sad smile. "No. I don't, to be honest. But from her notebooks, it was was hard for her to deal with patients who suffered."

"Understood." And Jack really did. They drank their waters and nibbled at their sandwiches before turning back.

"Let's visit the graves," Kalino said. "I want to honor my family members."

They headed back and rejoined the group they were supposed to be with. At the nearby church which Father Damien had built, Jack stared at the small wrought-iron enclosure that held the graves of Father Damien, and his successor, Father Joseph Dutton. Jack wasn't surprised to see the saint's grave covered in flowers. "Once we got news he was being canonized, the country of Belgium, where he was from, well, they insisted on digging up his remains," Kalino said. "For over a hundred years he was here, where he belonged. And they took him back. We let him go, but the authorities bent to public pressure and returned his right hand."

Kalino's eyes moistened. "We don't mind. His hand was all we needed. His hand healed. His hand helped. Even though he was gone long before my family came here and none of us met him, we still love him. We have benefitted from his incredible compassion. Nobody was an outcast in his mind. Nobody deserved to live alone, unloved. That to me is a true Christian." He opened his backpack and gave them each a flower.

"Here," he said. "Give him a little bit of love and let him know he's not forgotten. That his sacrifice to help those around him is the true meaning of love."

Jack took his time placing his own flower, a pink plumeria, on the black stone headrest. He reached through the bars of the fence and left the fragrant bud as he said a silent prayer of thanks to the great saint. *Please look after my uncle for me. I'm sorry he never told me about this place. I'm glad I'm finally here.*

An odd thing happened. A hot, almost searing shot of pain shot through his forehead. He wobbled for a moment then felt a warm flush of peace ripple through him. *Oh, he's centering me.* Jack wasn't a fanciful, woo-woo-type of guy so all of this struck him as bizarre yet wonderful. He turned and found Kalino's gaze on him.

"Aloha," Kalino said, his voice soft.

"Aloha," Jack responded. Their gazes held. Jack was falling hard for the guy. He urged himself not to, but it was almost impossible.

They completed their tour, walking back to the bus. For the first time, Jack noticed the white painted rock near the entrance of the hospital. It read, "Peace to all who enter here."

And, as Kalino's hands briefly, gently, collided with his, Jack knew, he'd found himself, some peace at last.

"I need to kiss you." Kalino's words came out in hot, whispered gusts in Jack's ear. They mirrored the pleasant anguish Jack felt.

Jack smiled. He could get used to this. All of it.

CHAPTER TEN

Jack and Kalino made it back with minutes to spare for Mingo and Francois' arrival at six o'clock.

Kalino went to pick up Moke and Jack suddenly missed them both. *Damn. I gotta settle down here.* He still hadn't heard from George and hadn't responded to a second text. Maybe he changed his mind, He hoped so, and the thought relieved his mind.

Moke ran to the front door as Jack opened it and threw himself at Mingo and Francois.

Moke seemed so happy to have his tags attached to his new collar, he jingled them in Mingo's face.

Mingo laughed and stroked the dog's head. "You've got some nice jewelry there, young man."

Moke stood beside Jack as Mingo and Francois greeted him.

Jack liked them immediately, the way they stopped moving, knelt down and gave Moke a lot of love.

"He's a keeper," Francois said. He unleashed a beautiful, toothy smile on Jack and shook his hand. He hugged Kalino who in turn, hugged Mingo.

Jack wasn't sure what he'd expected from Francois, but the tall, dark, muscular, handsome black man with the deep French accent was as sexy as all hell. Dressed in jeans and a puffy black, sleeveless jacket over a white T-shirt, he was all smiles, but his sharp gaze darted everywhere. He moved around the house making notes on his cell phone and snapping photos. He even touched the spot on the wall where the ants had been.

Francois stroked the area with a frown and muttered, "Hmph."

Mingo also wore jeans and an aloha shirt. He'd brought donuts from a bakery on the mainland and Kalino made coffee.

"Well?" Jack finally asked, anxious now.

"It's an easy house to wire." Francois stood in the kitchen with the others and picked up a pink-frosted donut. He bit into it. "I can put in hidden cameras. You do know you've had some uh, psyshic interference here, right?"

"Say what?" Jack's throat closed tight. He gripped the donut in his hand a little harder.

"Yeah. That wall there. I think the dog took care of it. But I'd ask a kahuna to come here and bless the house after we've put in some security measures. I'd like to change the lock on the front door, too. You need a dead bolt."

Jack swallowed over the piece of donut stuck in his throat. "Okay."

"Otherwise, pretty straightforward." Francois waved his donut around. "I can do everything tonight. Maybe you and Mingo can take a walk and discuss your other problem. Kalino, you wanna help me here?"

"Sure." Kalino washed his hands.

Moke seemed torn between which two men he should stay with but chose Jack and Mingo, who walked outside into the darkened backyard.

"Your friend George did not receive the apartment in New York, unlike what he told you."

Jack almost tripped over a large stone. "He didn't?"

Mingo sat on a low-lying wall from the property next door. Jack sat beside him, Moke flopping on his feet.

"I spoke to Edward Diamond. He's had a hard time contacting you because George told him he had no idea where you were."

Jack squinted at him in the darkness. "That's ridiculous! I don't believe it. Why would he lie to him?"

"Didn't want to face reality. In fact, the only property George gets is the one on the island of Oahu. That house is worth three million dollars, easy. Maybe more with the market being so hot right now. He also got a hundred thousand dollars in cash and a few pieces of art, which, if he sells them, should bring in around quarter of a million dollars. About a year ago, George signed a quit claim to this house and can never come after you for it.

"I've checked and he cannot sue you for the apartment in New York. Your uncle had both of you in his will until about a year ago when he removed George and made you and Edward his main inheritors."

"I didn't know any of this." Jack was stunned.

"You both get the New York apartment and all the other things in it." Mingo paused. "You get this house and car, and the dog. He even left funds with a local vet for his care."

"And yet George and his boyfriend dumped Moke." Jack reached down to touch the dog. Make gave his fingers a hearty lick.

Mingo's voice turned grave and quiet. "I know. And um, he left you the contents of his bank account here in the islands which is about half a million dollars. Edward gets the bank account in New York which is around the same."

"That's a lot of money." Jack was surprised.

"The publishing company is basically bankrupted. George emptied the bank account the moment he arrived. It had about seventy-five thousand dollars in it. We can go after him for those funds, or I can help you draft a letter which allows him to keep the money, and he must sign another quit claim form saying on condition that he gives you all the passwords to the online company accounts, all social media, credit cards,

bank account information, including the checkbook he's stolen, you won't sue him."

"He did all that?"

"According to the police, your uncle reported the company
checkbook stolen weeks ago, but declined to pursue it when
he realized it was George who took it."

Jack blew out a sigh. "Unbelievable."

"Your uncle canceled some accounts. Others he didn't. I
can help you with all of that."

Tears pricked the back of Jack's eyes. "I appreciate anything and everything you can do for me."

Mingo reached over and squeezed his shoulder. "It's
gonna be all right, Jack. Really. Death sucks, and families,
well, it can bring out the worst in them."

"That's the truth." Jack took another breath. "I just can't
believe my uncle is gone."

"I understand. You're here now. And you'll find Molokai
is a very healing place. You'll feel your uncle on the breeze.
He'll be a whisper on the wind, a shimmering star in the sky."

"You're so poetic. Are you sure you're an accountant?"

Mingo laughed. "Oh, yeah. But I'm a Hawaiian man, first
and foremost."

Jack nodded. "I see." He paused. "What do you know
about *Molokai molelo*?"

"Something like it helped me find Francois," Mingo said.
"Trust it. That spirit voice will never steer you wrong."

Inside the house, Kalino made himself feeding Moke something from a casserole dish on the kitchen floor.

"What's that?" Jack peered inside the container. Whatever
it was, it smelled rich and fragrant, and made Jack hungry for
much more than donuts.

Moke kept his head down, eating in the frantic way he had
since Jack had found him.

Kalino knelt beside Moke, giving him an indulgent smile. "My mom just stopped by. It's her special meal for dogs. Chicken, eggs, blueberries, apples, yellow squash, peas, zuccini, and sweet potatoes. Some people add broccoli but I think it makes dogs fart."

Jack burst out laughing. "She makes this for your dog?"

"Sure she does. Good, healthy, wholesome food. No additives. No muck. She'll give you the recipe if you like."

Moke finished the food and glanced at the casserole dish.

"He should have a third of this twice a day, but he's had half already. Give him the rest in the morning."

"Okay. And thanks. I really appreciate it." Jack reached out and touched Kalino's cheek. "I mean it."

"I know you do." Kalino rubbed his face against Jack's hand, then got to his feet. Moke whined when Kalino capped the container and put it in the fridge. "You can heat this up for thirty seconds in the morning, but he shouldn't eat it hot."

"I'll remember that, thanks." Jack was shocked to see that the fridge was filled with food.

"Listen, I have to say, I was impressed with the way you you didn't freak out when Francois mentioned dark magic had been worked here."

Jack shrugged. "Yeah. Well, I guess I should call a kahuna, but where do I find one?"

Kalino stared at him. "I'll ask my mom. You'll be okay till we find one for you. You'll get the real deal here. If black magic happened here, it would have been the work of an *Anā'anā* kahuna priest. I the old days, they could pray you to death."

Jack stared at him. "Can they still do that?"

"I don't know. I guess they could, but if that's what happened here, Francois said it was neutralized." Kalino bit his lip for a second. "But you weren't shocked and upset."

"Nah. I've been having experiences lately that make me

realize there's more to this life than the ah, everyday."

"What sort of experiences?"

Jack blew out a breath. "I don't even know how to describe them. My uncle's come to me a couple of times."

Kalino's face brightened. "But that's wonderful."

"I see a rainforest sometimes." Jack was reluctant to say more.

"Okay. I know all about the rainforest. Oh, man. Well, it sounds like you're vibing with this island already."

They grinned at one another then Kalino stepped forward and kissed him.

Their earlier encounter had been no fluke. Or a figment of Jack's imagination. They kissed with total abandon, Moke flopping himself on the floor with a sigh.

"Your dog's a drama queen," Kalino murmured against Jack's lips, making him laugh.

Jack had never experienced the kind of slow burn Kalino subjected him to. Their kisses went on for an hour, followed by some dry humping on the sofa that made Jack feel like a teenager all over again. They rolled around until Jack lay underneath Kalino whose body seemed to fit his perfectly. Jack held Kalino's head closer, yearning for deeper contact.

"You got rubbers?" Kalino asked as the night grew darker, and the only light seemed to come from Kalino's intense gaze. He rubbed his hard cock against Jack's, making them both moan.

"I think I brought everything else in the world except those." Jack shifted a little. Kalino was rigid against his thigh.

"Well, we can do other things." Kalino's gleeful expression made Jack laugh.

"I'll follow your lead."

"Yeah, you will." Kalino rolled off him and moved to the floor, kneeling beside Jack. He undid Jack's pants, shoved down his underpants, which wasn't easy with Jack so erect, and with an expert touch, took Jack's swollen cock into his hands and mouth.

Jack let out a cry as Kalino took his time, savoring him, tasting the first beads of moisture on the tip of Jack's leaking shaft. Suddenly, he felt drops of liquid on his face. He opened his eyes. Man, oh, man. He was back in the forest. The earth and lush green plants were wet.

"You feel it too?" Kalino asked.

"Yeah. Oh, yeah." Jack touched Kalino's face as his mouth moved back over Jack's length. Kalino was wet, too.

What's happening to me? Jack had never experienced anything like this. His spirit was doing somersaults and as Kalino's mouth tightened, Jack gasped. Their extensive playtime had robbed him of any will to hold on, to keep himself from coming.

He rode the wave hard and fast, Kalino's fingers and tongue wrapped around him, urging him on. Jack wished it had lasted longer, but he also wanted to pleasure Kalino, too.

Kalino rose and took Jack's hand. Getting to his feet, Jack let him lead the way to the bedroom where Kalino finished undressing Jack and allowed Jack to remove his clothes too.

They fell on the bed and Jack became aware of the smell of some kind of blossom.

"Night jasmine," Kalino whispered in his ear. "Right outside the window. Lovely, isn't it?"

"Uh, huh." Jack focused on the beautiful man lying beside him, thrilled to see how big and hard Kalino's cock was for him. Jack stroked it with his tongue only.

"Torturer," Kalino whispered, passing a hand across his eyes.

"I just got started." Jack hadn't experienced anything so languid and lovely in a long time and enjoyed working Kalino up to a magnificent explosion.

Just as Kalino got close to coming, Jack moved off him, but

Kalino went nuts, grabbing Jack's head.

"Oh, no, no. Oh, no." Kalino batted his cock against Jack's smiling lips and Jack took in his length again, slowly, enjoying every second of Kalino's eruption.

When he came, Jack wondered if any store was open so he could buy an industrial size box of condoms.

"Come here, stud," Kalino whispered, pulling Jack into his arms. "I've got plenty of rubbers at home."

Jack gaped at him. How did he do that? How did Kalino always know what he was thinking?

He gave himself up to Kalino's kisses and snuggled against him.

Later, much later, he awakened. It was eleven o'clock and he had to peel himself out of Kalino's arms to take Moke outside.

The air was fragrant, the night blooming jasmine filling his senses. Moke ran into the backyard and did his thing, Jack just able to make out the dog's form in the dark. He'd never been in a place this quiet, or this perfect.

A noise behind him made him turn.

His naked lover was there, smiling at him. "There you are. I missed you."

"I missed you, too," Jack said. And realized he meant he'd been missing Kalino Garcia Jr. his whole entire life.

When Kalino left for work the next morning, Jack got up feeling better than he had for ages. He loved that he could linger in the quiet of the day over coffee and eat whatever he could find in the fridge. He might even have one of Mingo's donuts. He'd left them there for Jack. He rummaged for the leftover chicken casserole for Moke then found it on the kitchen benchtop along with a note, and oh joy, a loaf of fresh coconut bread and a can of condensed milk.

The note read, *"You could nuke the casserole but it's better just to leave it out at room temperature. It should be perfect temp by the time you get up. You snore and it's cute! Some ants came into the kitchen but I told them to go away. See you later!"*

Jack was incensed. *I don't snore!* Then he reread the part about the ants. Was it a joke? He wasn't sure, but Moke was pacing, so he fed him. Moke demolished his meal in a few bites. Time to get some dog food, or Mrs. Garcia's recipe.

It made Jack feel good to know he'd met someone so nurturing. All his life he'd taken care of himself, now he thought about it. His parents had been loving, but distant, then cruel, especially when he came out to them.

But as a kid, his mom had rented out rooms to a revolving door of artists and writers in their Chelsea brownstone. Breakfast was the only meal she'd felt obliged to supply and that involved leaving boxes of cereal and bowls of fruit on the kitchen table, and milk in the fridge. Everybody helped themselves.

She left money in Jack's room for his school lunches weekdays, and on the weekends, he was usually over at Cameron's.

Jack got into the habit there of waking up early and taking the cash Cameron left in an antique snuff box in the hall closet. He'd walk over to the bodega at the corner and buy the morning paper, bagels, coffee, milk, and juice.

By the time he returned to the apartment, Cameron and George were up and about ready to brew one of their endless pots of coffee.

Jack couldn't resist the urge to smile hugely at the thought of Kalino bringing a casserole for his dog and fresh bread and milk for Jack.

Who does that? Kalino does. If I'm dreaming, I don't want to wake up. He is yummy.

Jack sliced up the bread and dipped it into the milk, eating over the kitchen sink. He downed two cups of coffee and stared out of the window at the adorable red-capped cardinals playing on the sill. Beside him, Moke's gaze fell on them, but then returned to the rapidly disappearing loaf.

Grinning at Moke, Jack decided they would take a long, long walk along the winding trail that had once been the private path of the great Queen Ka'ahumanu.

And now, another queen enjoys it! Jack didn't bother with a shower. He wanted to keep the scent of Kalino on his skin. Earthy, spicy, with a touch of coconut. That was how Kalino smelled. Besides, he'd need a good, hot shower after his walk.

Man and dog took a few appreciative breaths outside the house and made their way along the road to where Jack had read the trail started. After a two-mile hike, they found the place. Moke sat at the edge of the creek, and watched Jack swim.

After several minutes, and a lot of coaxing, Moke stepped into the water and appeared to love it. He drank and swam and barked at a dragonfly that hovered too close to him. Jack laughed. He found the whole experience so peaceful he wasn't surprised that old-time writers said this had been the queen's sanctuary. The water was so clear and clean, Jack felt he had to be dreaming, and together he and Moke walked home wet.

Jack took a shower as Moke rolled around on a couple of clean towels.

"Goofball." Jack stroked the dog's belly and promised him he'd be back shortly. He drove to the market, stocked up on basic staples for him and Moke and returned to the house.

Moke was just inside the front door, looking frantic. Jack wondered why. He hadn't been gone long.

Somebody's been here. Man. This poor little guy is shaking.

Jack's cell phone rang. He checked the screen. It was Kalino.

"Hey, handsome," Kalino said. "Why don't you come by the store? I have a shake for you and some food for Moke. My mom made it for him."

"Oh, you do? How cool are you! You spoil us. Both of us.

Thank you for the bread and milk."

"Spoil you? I've only just begun."

Jack couldn't help grinning. It would never have occurred to Robert to make him a shake or leave fresh bread for him, or — *stop it. It's over with him.*

The doorbell rang. "We'll be there soon," Jack said. "I think we've got company."

"Okay." Kalino seemed distracted. Jack heard voices. Customers. They ended the call and Jack went to the door. He was surprised to see Kalino Garcia Sr. and an elderly man who seemed fit and energetic. He bounced inside his new-looking white sneakers, his brown legs and arms sprouting from red shorts and a billowing red shirt.

"This is the kahuna." Kalino Sr. jerked his thumb toward the man whose long gray hair had been held back in a bun. "He come to fix your house. You finish the casserole? Can I take the dish? You want the recipe?"

Jack knew the kahuna was scrutinizing him. He felt intimidated because his insides suddenly seemed liquid. His face felt like it was on fire.

"Yes. Thank you." Jack's voice felt like it was coming from some place else. He became aware of Moke trembling at his side.

"Who's been in here?" The kahuna stepped inside and walked straight over to the wall where Moke had peed. "You're giving this dog a lot of work trying to protect you." The kahuna shook a finger at Kalino Sr. "This is worse than your son thought."

Kalino Sr.'s brows flew up into his hairline. He went to the kitchen and returned with the casserole dish.

"But I didn't get to wash it yet." Jack came out of whatever haze the kahuna had put him in.

"No *huhu*. No worries. This more important." He walked out the door in a big hurry and closed the door behind him.

141

Suddenly, he opened it again. "You do whatever he says."

"I will. Thank you." *I think.*

When they were alone, the kahuna bent and stroked Moke's head. "Good boy," he said over and over. He straightened and looked at Jack, grave concern etched in his lined face.

"Do you have any idea who tried to curse you?"

Jack was so taken aback he didn't know how to respond. "Somebody curse me? Wow. The only one I can think of is my uncle's former lover, George."

"George." The kahuna bent his head and seemed to roll the name around his tongue and brain for a minute. Then came words that were not English but felt powerful and old.

With a shock, Jack realized it was raining now. Thunder and lightning crackled over the house.

The dog whined and Jack reached out to touch him.

"This George . . . he hired an *Anā'anā* kahuna. You know what that is?"

"A dark priest?"

"Yes. But for this magic to work it requires a direct line of sight." The kahuna paused. "He paid a lot of money but it didn't work. He worked against you. And your uncle." He paused. "Oh. Your poor uncle." His eyes filled with tears. "You must never be near this man George again."

"Okay."

"Now. I can help you." The kahuna pointed to the dog. "I can help you both. But you can never speak of this to anyone. What I do is good magic. Good healing. It is secret work, born of love."

"I understand." Jack's urge to run screaming from the house subsided and he started feeling better when the rain stopped. "But how do I repay you for this? How much do you charge?"

The old man looked at him. "I want the blood of your first-born child."

"What?" Jack gaped at him.

The kahuna started laughing, bent over double, slapping his thighs and pointing at Jack. "Your face! You should see your face!"

Jack shook his head.

"I will charge you a hundred dollars. Is that okay?" The old man seemed anxious now.

"Wow. That's all?"

"That's all. I don't like black magic. I don't like cruel people. Now how much salt do you have in the house? You'll need to take salt baths for the next three weeks."

"Okay. I don't think there's much here now but I can get some."

"And before we start, you must promise never to tell anybody, I mean *anybody* what we do here today."

"I promise," Jack said as a sudden crack of thunder hit the house, seeming to make it shake.

"Good," the kahuna said. "Now go get whatever salt you have."

CHAPTER ELEVEN

Jack thought he dreamed the entire ceremony, especially when the kahuna seemed to open the wall in Jack's living room and they glimpsed a raging volcano and floods of fire in a dark, dank cavern.

"What the hell?" Jack could barely breathe from the heat. The kahuna sweated and kept chanting, throwing salt and water and waving burning pieces of sweetgrass around.

"*Oli Pale. Noho ana ke akua,*" he chanted over and over.

Jack had no idea what it meant. He recognized the word *akua*, the Hawaiian word for God, from his reseach into Kalaupapa. The chant must have worked because the volcano vanished, leaving only smoke and acrid water. Jack choked. The dog choked.

"Good," the kahuna said with a smug smile. "That didn't take long. He's an amateur." He turned to Jack, an odd look on his face. "Did this George introduce you to somebody called Kevin?"

Jack gaped once again at him. "Yeah. He said he was a publisher."

"Phhhth. He's no publisher. He's a wannabe kahuna. He's been in here." He pointed to the floor. "Under the foundations. You need to get that blocked off." He held a hand over the floor then pointed to the right. "The passage way is hidden. Oh. I see it in my mind. Hidden by a fake compost heap on that side of the house."

Jack stared at him. There was a fake compost heap? "Thank you. I'll call Francois right away."

"Yes. Good. The security man. I like him." The kahuna stepped away from the mess before him and it all disappeared. The living room wall was back and all of it could have been a dream, except for the burning smell. And the searing heat underneath Jack's feet.

"Kevin was here?" Jack asked.

"Yeah. I recognize his work. You should feel lucky his powers are limited. But he charged this George plenty to work against you. *Plenty!* Thousands! I know you will feel great anger in the coming weeks but you must not retaliate. Or speak of it."

"I won't. I promise you that."

"Good." Apparently, it was the kahuna's favorite word. "The smell will go away. Maybe a day or two. Let it drift away on its own. Don't do anything to interfere with the natural process. You can open a window, but don't spray room freshener or anything."

"I won't."

"Good." The kahuna stared at him. "I'll leave you a braid of sweetgrass. Burn it at night for spirit protection and open up the windows. It'll help. And one more thing. This is all over money. So you must be vigilant."

Jack stared at him, astonished. How did the old man know so much?

"You will know this clearing has been done when you see the *oloma'o.*"

"And what's that?"

"You'll see." And the kahuna smiled at him.

Jack wrote down the word *oloma'o* after the kahuna spelled it for him. He Googled it on his cell phone. It was a local bird, a beautiful little brown, black and gray thing, endemic to Molokai, and, unfortunately, according to te report he read, 'probably extinct.' *Great, just great. How am I supposed to see such a rare creature?*

He couldn't worry about that now. He'd lost track of time,

though upon checking, it had only been an hour since he'd spoken to Kalino. It seemed like an eternity.

He went outside to get a look at the compost heap he'd never even noticed, but all he saw was a massive black box that almost looked like a square cauldron. It had the stench of rotting food, though there was nothing in it now.

"Come on boy," he said to his trusty sidekick.

He locked up the house and made sure the window locks were in place. If Kevin chose to return in his absence, there was nothing he could do about it.

He and Moke drove to the market to load up on the strange collection of things Jack would require over the next few days. The cashier didn't bat an eyelid when Jack asked for all the red salt she had. She handed him five bags of four-pound red Hawaiian salt.

"You having a luau?" she asked. "Everybody uses the salt for the kalua pork."

"Something like that." He picked up a package of powdered kava kava. He would mix it with water and drink the mixture to alleviate stress and anxiety, and also help him sleep if he needed it. Kahuna's orders. Next, he loaded up on a bag containing a hundred tea light candles and a box of matches.

He could tolerate salt baths and endless white candles being kept lit in all the windows, but Jack's head was spinning at the notion that Kevin was some kind of evil sorcerer. He looked so . . . ordinary. Now that he thought about it, George had been cagey about Kevin's identity. Jack had assumed there was a romantic interest there. He never would have *dreamed* black magic was involved.

And Kevin might have had limited powers, but *dang*. He had them. Jack's kahuna said whatever malevolence he'd flung at Jack would rebound on him—and George—threefold. The idea made Jack shiver.

Once he'd picked up his much-needed items and a bag of dry dog food, he stowed them in the trunk and greeted Moke who waited patiently in the front passenger seat for him.

"Wanna visit Kalino?" Jack asked.

Moke's ears went up in a defininte sign of agreement. He licked Jack's face as they drove away.

They made the short trip, parked, and wandered over to the Molokai Mule Café. Jack loved the confident way the dog strode inside.

"Hey cutie!" a woman's voice called out. Annie.

Jack was happy to see her and Lee, but was disappointed to learn they were leaving the island.

"We'll be in touch. I've already started putting notes together on my aunt's book," she said. "Do you Skype, Jack?"

"Sure I do. I have Zoom, too." He caught Kalino's searing gaze and wondered if he would be allowed to kiss him.

"Here are my deets." Annie handed Jack a business card.

"I'll email you," he promised her.

She stood, hugging Jack, then Moke, then Kalino.

Moke slipped behind the counter to lap at a bowl of water. Jack heard him wolfing down something.

"He ate his lunch in record time," Kalino said. "Don't you feed him?"

Jack shrugged. "I do, but he's catching up."

"Don't worry. I just enjoy making fun of you."

They waved goodbye to Lee and Annie.

"Make fun of this," Jack said, pulling Kalino into his arms.

Kalino gave him a swift kiss but pulled away again. "Not here. Not in public. People are weird about that sort of thing on this island."

"Sorry."

He touched Jack's cheek. "But in private nothing can stop me." He gazed into Jack's eyes. "You smell of sulphur. Rotten eggs. I guess the kahuna found you. Here, you'll need this.

Extra protein for you. It'll help keep you grounded after the clearing you just went through."

Jack grinned, even though he didn't think smelling like rotten eggs was particularly sexy, and took the shake Kalino offered him.

Moke nosed around his now-empty dishes, then came and settled at Jack's feet.

"I might go home and take a nap," Jack said.

"Oh, I wish I could join you." Kalino looked so sad, Jack wanted to kiss him again, but resisted.

"Why don't you come by after work?" Jack suggested.

"I'll do that." Kalino looked happy again.

Back home, the landline was ringing. The old-fashioned handset had no function to display call waiting, so it was a surprise to find George on the other end of the line.

As soon as Jack answered, George snarled, "Your uncle took everything from me. And now you're doing it, too. You found the damned diary! That thing brought nothing but disaster for Cameron. I hope it ruins your life, too. We'll see how much he likes the truth coming out about him. We'll see how much you likes having your new assets frozen . . . I hate him. I hate you both!"

Jack sat for a moment, shocked by the tirade. "What's going on?" he asked. But George had ended the call. A few minutes later, Jack got a call from Mingo McCloud.

Jack quickly explained everything that had been going on, without going into any detail about the kahuna's spiritual clearing.

"Don't worry," Mingo said. "It's my job to worry. George knows we're onto him. I've frozen all of your uncle's accounts that George had access to. You have full access to the account in New York that Cameron left you. But all the ones here, George keeps dipping into. At least, he was until an hour ago.

He's gone berserk. I fully believe he intended to fleece the accounts for every last penny. Cameron left him well-off. But I guess for some people, there's never enough money. He keeps trying to cash checks but your uncle reported them stolen weeks ago. George deposited three checks for huge amounts yesterday, and the bank returned them. He apparently went in there today and tried to cash another one. When he realized they wouldn't accept it and the other checks wouldn't clear, he blew a fuse."

"Oh, that explains his meltdown," Jack said.

"I'm emailing you a copy of the letter I want to send to George. With your approval, I'll have it delivered to him and I guarantee when he realizes we really can and will prosecute him, he'll sign the agreement and we'll get him off your back. We're going to reorganize everything and make sure Cameron's wishes are followed to the letter."

"Thanks," Jack said, feeling better about things now.

On the other end of the line, Mingo was talking to somebody with an unmistakable French accent.

"Francois says he is coming there today to seal the crawlspace under your house," Mingo said. "And I've been thinking. You really shouldn't talk to George at all. Maybe you should change the landline number. Just make sure you give it to me."

"Great." Jack felt Mingo seemed reassuring but he hated the idea that George was out for revenge.

"George can't do any of the things he threatened you with," Mingo continued. "You're listed in the probate court as the executor of the estate. Edward Diamond's been a little hard to get hold of, but I'll keep trying. You'll have to settle things between you on the matter of your uncle's New York apartment."

"Right." Another headache. Jack wished he didn't have to deal with any of it, but he was grateful he wouldn't have to worry about money after a lifetime of constantly stressing about it.

Jack was apprehensive, in spite of Mingo's assurances. "I have no idea where George is and he makes me nervous. I'm afraid to leave my house. I'm afraid to leave my dog here on his own. What it he comes here in the middle of the night?" There. It was a relief just to say it.

"He won't."

"How do you know that? We don't know where he is. I keep expecting him to jump out at me from around a tree or something."

"Oh, but I know where he is. He's in Honolulu."

"Mingo, how in the world do you know that?"

"I'm a master sleuth. Didn't you know that?" A pause, then Mingo chuckled. "His Facebook page. He's at the House Without a Key drinking cocktails. His post says, 'It's five o'clock somewhere.' Man, he has ugly feet."

"Facebook?" Jack almost laughed. "I have no web presence. Or any desire to splash my daily activities all over the internet."

"Keep it that way. The less George knows about your activities, the better. Now get your number changed. Pronto, Tonto."

They ended their call and Jack called the phone company. He'd have a new number in twenty-four hours. He jotted it down and made a note to give it to Francois, Mingo, and Kalino. In the meantime, he'd answer no calls and just use his cell phone. At least on that, he could see who was calling him.

Jack began the process the kahuna had commanded. Candles lit, olive oil dotting the surface of each, he repeated the Hawaiian chant of protection he'd written down, certain he was mangling the beautiful language. It couldn't be helped. But he hoped the ancestral spirits knew his efforts were sincere.

As the late afternoon sky darkened, Jack made coffee for himself and fed Moke some dry food. The dog looked up at him as though he were crazy.

Moke wouldn't look at it, and refused to eat it.

Jack sighed. "I left your new casserole at the café, sorry boy. Maybe Kalino will bring it home for you."

He called Kalino but a woman answered the café phone and said he was busy. "Call back," she hollered over the cacophany of noise.

Jack texted instead, asking if Kalino could bring the casserole over with him when he finished work.

He took his dog, cell phone, and coffee outside. Moke snuggled close as they lounged on an old outdoor sofa that had seen better centuries. Drowsy now, Jack felt bereft because he did not feel or smell the jungle. And he missed Kalino. He must have dozed off though, because he was awakened by a loud hammering at the front door.

Jack couldn't believe the panic he felt. *I was never this much of a nervous wreck in New York. Why am I so nuts now? Because a treasured friend tried to curse me.*

He opened the door wishing he had a gun and was relieved to see Francois.

"You okay? You look pale," Francois said. Next to him, anyone did. He was a tall, good looking chunk of dark chocolate, that man.

Without waiting for a response, Francois walked inside and pressed a huge box of donuts into Jack's hands.

"Mingo says you need the sugar. So eat up."

"Wow. Thanks."

Francois was lost in his world now, moving around the house, Moke in tow, checking the cameras and security setup.

"Looks good. I've got two guys outside now, putting some siding into place to make sure your intruder can't get back in again. Do you want to keep the compost container? It's got a creepy vibe. I say we haul it away."

"Haul away," Jack said. "Please."

"Any sign of trouble, call the police. Your system has a phone function that calls right over there. You just press the numbers nine and nine on your phone once you're in the app."

He sat at the table in the living room, showing Jack how to operate the system. He kept blinking and sniffing.

"It smells like crap in here," he announced. "Gotta go." And he left.

Five minutes later, Francois returned, a look of fury on his face. "My guys found a tape recorder under the house and evidence of a bad ritual, but a lot of it's gone." He gazed at Jack before saying softly, "I think the kahuna took what he could but left the tape recorder in case I needed evidence. I'll take it with me but I'd say it hasn't been in use for a while."

"What do you think it was used for?"

"I'm assuming it was used to record telephone conversations but the wires were cut. I don't see the cord going anywhere. Maybe your uncle found it, or someone else did and cut the wires and left everything there because even touching the product of island magic can bring heaps of bad luck."

"And you're okay with handling it?"

Francois gazed at him, his eyes sparkling with mischief. "Oh, yes. I'll listen to the tape and if there's anything you need to know, I'll report back to you. And don't forget to eat some donuts. Sugar is a good antidote to bad juju."

"Well, thank you. And thank Mingo for me, too, please." Jack tried to loosen his shoulders and neck. "Is there any other stuff, ah, still down there?"

"Nope. And I'll make sure what we took is destroyed. Don't think about it anymore. I just wanted you to know." Francois suddenly grinned. "You need to plant red ti plants where the compost was. It's a highly protective plant spiritually and a lot prettier than that yucky bin. Anyway, you have a good night. Lock up after me, yeah?"

"I will. And thanks again."

On their own again, Jack and Moke checked the contents of the fridge. Moke got the last of a piece of chicken, Jack got a glazed pineapple donut from yesterday's box. He had a whole new box to indulge in at his leisure. He took a second donut, just to be polite.

They returned to the sofa on the lanai and fell asleep once again, Moke's head nestled against Jack's thigh.

He had no idea how long he slept, but it was a dreamless sleep, which was probably a good thing. But he awakened to the sound of someone bashing at the front door.

"Thank God," Kalino said, when Jack opened it. He had a pizza box with a plastic, lidded dish atop of it. "I've been knocking for several minutes."

Jack kissed him and led him inside.

Moke must have known the plastic dish was for him and pranced as Kalino emptied it into his dish in the kitchen.

Outside, in the Molokai night, deer barked, an owl hooted, and then came a light rain.

"The house feels weird," Kalino said. "I'm not leaving you here alone." He gestured to the candle on the window sill. "I see you're busy following the kahuna's orders."

Jack said nothing.

"Let's have dinner. I don't suppose we can watch a movie because you don't have TV. I wonder what we can do instead." Kalino's wild cackle of laughter broke the tension between them.

"I have my laptop. We can watch Netflix. Oh, no. I won't have internet until tomorrow. And my cell phone's too small for us to watch movies." For a moment, Jack felt defeated.

"Are you okay?" Kalino asked.

"I'm fine. Now." Jack reached for him. "I'll buy a TV, I promise."

"I don't care about TV. I quite like being with a caveman."

"A caveman? I like that." Jack kissed him. "I hope you came prepared."

"Prepared? You mean, did I bring food?"

Jack touched Kalino's dear face. "No. Not food."

"What then?" Kalino laughed. "Oh, you mean this?" He whipped out a foil packet from his back pocket.

"You brought one? Just one condom?"

"How many did you think we'd use?" Before Jack could respond, Kalino pulled him closer and kissed him. He pulled back again. "You know it stinks like hell in here, right?"

"Um. Yeah." Jack tried to clear the lusty thoughts from his brain.

"So, we'll take it outside." Kalino began removing Jack's clothes and Jack took off Kalino's. Soon they were naked and Kalino held Jack's cock with both hands, gazing into his eyes.

"You, me, jiggy-jiggy," he said, making Jack laugh.

He led him to the backyard, Moke romping out there with them. In the quiet cool, he sniffed around the yard, chasing who knew what, then flopping on the grass, rolling on his back. Jack knew just how he felt, all happy and trusting.

He groped for Kalino's cock. The two men kissed, Jack wondering how it was that his neighbor wasn't outside watering his garden. Or at least, pretending to water it.

"I've never been here without that guy watering," Kalino whispered in his ear.

Damn. How does he keep reading my mind?

"But in case he is, let's give him a good show." Kalino bent and took Jack's cock into his mouth, gripping his ass cheeks to bring him closer.

Jack bit off a moan. He didn't want to encourage his neighbor to come out and watch.

Kalino worked on him at a fast pace, as though he couldn't

wait, which worked up Jack's appetite too. He couldn't wait to fuck Kalino. Kalino came off Jack and turned him around so that he was kneeling on the lanai sofa.

Jack held his breath. It had been a long time since anyone had rimmed him. He'd forgotten the sheer pleasure of having a man's tongue on his ass, working its way down to his cock and balls. Kalino knelt between Jack's parted thighs and licked his hole like it was his last meal on earth.

The sensations building up in Jack sent him to the moon. He arched his back and raised his head to the sky. *Yes! This feels amazing. He's sending my soul to the very moon hovering over us now.*

Jack let out a moan. *How did I live without passion for so long?* He blinked, trying to blot out the memories of fast and often unsatisfying sex with his ex.

He mentally shook the thoughts free and focused on Kalino, who got up beside Jack and pulled him onto his lap. Kalino bit off a corner of the rubber and extracted it with gentle fingers.

"I gotta fuck you," he said. "Get on on me. Now."

"Wait. What?"

Kalino wriggled around until he had enough room to glove up.

"Why do I have to bottom?" Jack asked.

"I brought the condoms. My rubbers. My cock. My choice."

"Oh."

"Next time, come prepared, Jack."

Next time. Jack loved the sound of that. "You brought more?" he asked as he positioned himself over Kalino's lap. He lowered himself onto Kalino's hard shaft, both of them letting out gasps as he slowly entered Jack.

"Oh, God." Once Jack became used to Kalino's sheer size inside him he moved up and down, riding him hard and fast. Kalino planted his feet on the ground harder and held Jack's ass with one hand, using the other to stroke Jack along with their mutual thrusts.

It had been so long that Jack couldn't hold it. Kalino was right behind him, coming a minute after Jack did. Kalini released Jack's cock and lifted his fingers to his lips, licking them.

"You taste amazing."

Jack kept Kalino inside him, moving around on his lap. "There's more where that came from."

"Good. Because I've got about six boxes for us." He grinned and kissed Jack again. "They'll just fit in the bathroom with all those tubes of toothpase you have."

Jack laughed. "So, you noticed?"

"I notice everything. And the more I see, the more I like." He lifted Jack off him. "Shower, then bed, okay? We'll burn some sweetgrass. That'll help the smell."

Later, much later, in the middle of a colorful dream, Jack became aware of an odd smell and Moke whining. And then, Kalino shaking him awake.

"Wha . . . What is it?" Jack opened an eye, peering into the darkness. A shadowy figure stood at the foot of the bed. "Who the hell is that?"

"I don't know 'cause I never met him, but I think it's your dead uncle," Kalino said. "I'll leave you two alone."

CHAPTER TWELVE

Uncle Cameron shimmered into sharper view and Jack's eyes filled with tears.

"I'm sorry my darling. But you're protected now. I'm sorry he did this to you. But please, don't hurt George. He's a sick and dangerous man. Karma will get him." A long pause. "In the end."

"Why would you think I'd try and hurt him?"

"Because he is trying to hurt you. He hasn't been the easiest partner I could have picked."

"I don't want you to be dead," Jack blurted. He stared at the ghostly shape before him. Uncle Cameron looked pretty good. For a dead guy.

"Death is just another room. That's all. Think of me as being in another room. Oh, Jack, be happy. Please. You have the power and means to do whatever you want now."

Over Uncle Cameron's shoulder, Jack glimpsed a woman walking toward him.

"Eliza! Is that you?" Jack could hardly believe his friend had found Uncle Cameron in the hereafter.

"It's me," she said. "And I love you."

She was whole and as beautiful as ever.

"We have to go," Cameron said, and with that, their images vanished.

"I love you both," Jack shouted into the ether. He was so glad to know that Eliza was okay. And he liked thinking of her and Cameron in another time and space, but very, very close. He should have been scared. Should have been freaked out. But there was something about this island, this house, that made mystic moments seem . . . normal.

"You okay?" Kalino asked from the door. He came in with two mugs of murky brown liquid. "It's kava kava."

"Oh, good. I wanted to try that."

Jack took one of the cups and leaned against their bunched-up pillows, sipping.

Kalino sat beside him, drinking his.

"You seemed pretty calm about my dead uncle dropping by for a visit," Jack said.

"Dead people are pretty common on Molokai. I've seen dead cowboys race past me and children singing in trees. Children that died long ago."

"Is everyone like that here?"

Kalino gave him a small smile. "No. So, what do you think of the kava kava?"

"It makes my lips tingle and the back of my throat, too."

"That means it's working. Drink up. We've gotta get some sleep."

It was the last thing Jack remembered until Kalino awakened him with kisses around six a.m.

"I've gotta go, babe. I'm taking Moke with me."

"No. Don't leave."

"It's only work. Once your phone and internet's all settled, come by and visit me."

"But why are you taking Moke?"

"He needs to play and be a dog. Pete misses him. Besides, the house stinks really bad this morning. My mom would love to have him for the day."

Jack couldn't argue with Moke having some fun. He, however, was condemned to another salt bath. The sulphuric smell wouldn't leave his skin no matter what he did, but he did feel relaxed afterward. *How the heck can Kalino stand to be near me when I smell like this?*

He felt so relaxed after the bath he wondered how much of that was the lingering effect of kava kava. He had so many questions he pondered calling the kahuna and asking for more help. Maybe he should try more kava kava instead. He passed on that idea since the packaging said to drink it later in the day. And yeah, now that he thought about it, he had gone right to sleep after drinking it in the middle of the night.

Jack wanted to savor the mellow feeling and decided to skip coffee. He cracked open a bottle of Hawaiian spring water and stepped outside into the backyard, hoping this would unlock the portal to his uncle again.

Nothing.

Jack sighed and sat on the old porch swing he still hadn't used. *I'll replace the swing and get a better sofa for out here.* He swung in silence for a few moments, drinking his water. He was used to being busy. Not used to being . . . alone. With nothing but himself.

It was pleasant, once he realized it was okay to do nothing. He'd watched an old episode of *The Dick Van Dyke Show* once and they'd talked about an Italian expression, *dolce far niente*, how sweet to do nothing.

I wonder if there is a Hawaiian version of that?

If he was going to stay here, he had to work on his next steps. That involved getting the house to work better for him. He needed internet and new outdoor furniture. And he had to learn the recipe for Moke's dog food.

Back in the kitchen, he wasn't surprised to find the dry dog food from Moke's bowl in the trash. Kalino must have tossed it before he left. That gave Jack an idea.

In the living room, he sat at the dining table and made a list of all the things he needed and wanted. He wrote and wrote, surprised when he glanced up at one point and saw in his mind a different living room all together. Before he proceeded, he checked his bank balance in New York—the one Cameron had left him. *Wow.* It was a lot of money.

He wasn't angry that Cameron hadn't helped his writing career. But his uncle's money would help others. Not just as a publisher, but he wanted to open up the house to a writing salon, say once a week. It would be the kind of literary salon European society held in the seventeenth and eighteenth centuries.

Jack's thoughts raced. In Britain, penny coffee houses opened everywhere in the eighteenth century. For a penny, people could attend literary and art salons, drink tea, coffee or hot chocolate, and listen to new stories, or observe art. *We could charge a penny admission and donate the money to charity. I'll have to ask Kalino if we can hold a theme night salon there once a month or something. Oh, man. I love this idea.*

He kept making notes, and then the landline phone rang. Jack answered it, hoping it wasn't George calling to scream at him again.

"Hi. Mr. Christie?" a male voice asked.

"Yes," Jack said, fearing trouble.

"It's Hawaiian Telecom. Just calling to tell you we've switched to your new number and a technician is on his way now to install your internet and cable connection for TV. Unless you want a dish."

Jack didn't remember asking for cable connection but the guy went on.

"The notes say you didn't want TV. Was that an error?"

"My error. Sorry about that. Can we go for a dish?"

"Yeah, but the dish won't go in until tomorrow, but I can start all the wiring for it."

"Great, thanks." Jack figured he'd need it if he intended on having slow nights with Kalino and Moke and a pizza. The idea warmed his heart. Within seconds, came a knock at the door. The guy who came inside seemed nervous.

"You burn some eggs or something?" he asked, glancing around at the lit candles.

"Something like that." Jack tried to give him a happy smile

but felt it only seemed to make the technician more wary. The guy didn't say much apart from examining the phone jack, then went outside.

Half an hour later, Jack had everything he needed apart from the satellite dish.

The technician handed him a card. "This is your new password."

Jack looked at it and laughed. *Scaryghost. How apt.*

The technician gestured toward the huge spool of white cable lying against the wall. "Our office will call you with the dish installation time. That's not my department. Sorry."

"No problem." Jack closed and locked the door. Once he was on his own again, Jack extinguished the candles. To him, the house smelled better. *But what do I know?* He checked his list for things to do. He needed plants. Lots of them. He should check out his new internet and figure out how to buy some furniture online. His instructions from the kahuna indicated he needed to take four salt baths a day. That could wait. In spite of everything he needed to do, instead, he called Kalino who urged him to come visit.

"I'll make you my best green chocolate shake, so hurry."

Jack laughed. Green chocolate? Sounded pretty good. He wanted to swing by the Garcia residence and pick up Moke but he could do that on his way home.

At the café, Kalino seemed pleased to see Jack but waved off his offer of help.

"Have your shake, then tell me about your day so far."

"What's in this?" Jack asked. The cup seemed heavy. It wasn't until he finished that Kalino told him it contained dark chocolate cocoa, half an avocado, kale, cucumber, coconut milk, a dash of almond butter and spirulina.

It had been damned tasty even though Jack hated kale.

"Great," he said, hoping he'd kept a poker face.

Jack went home, wondering why he felt so tired, then realized it was emotional exhaustion. The house smelled so bad he couldn't sleep inside, but went out and slept on the lanai, Moke lying right beside him. He fell into a deep sleep, troubled thoughts infiltrating visions of lush, green forests, and Kalino's beautiful face, smiling. Smiling just for him.

At one point, he heard voices. His neighbor. He couldn't rouse himself to speak. Moke licked his ear and man and dog slept again.

Jack had an awful dream that Moke died and was permanently in the forest with Cameron.

No! Not Moke. I need him here. With me.

In the dream, Moke was running, chasing, chattering in the forest.

Jack awoke abruptly, not sure what exactly had stirred him. Moke had burrowed even closer to Jack, who pulled the dog into his arms. Moke licked Jack's chin.

The sky seemed light. What time was it? He sat up, his back in agony. He yawned and stretched.

"Morning!" his cheery neighbor called out. "You've slept like a dead man since yesterday." He had his hose in hand and Jack gave him a friendly wave.

"Breakfast," Jack whispered to his dog, and Moke sprang like a fawn across the lanai.

They went back inside, where Moke supervised Jack preparing some freshly chopped chicken for the dog. He heard a knock at the front door. He almost fell over when he saw it was Kalino.

"Here . . . I brought you some bread . . . you know . . . just to be polite."

Jack stared at the shadows under the other man's eyes, sensed the indecision and the fear, and he pulled Kalino to him.

"You want to be polite? Try giving me one of these." His mouth found Kalino's, and he felt a charge of volcanic heat when Kalino's hand cupped the back of his head. Jack pressed him against the wall, and the two men kissed with such hunger, they had to break apart physically to breathe again.

Kalino was back in his arms seconds later, a bewildered look on his face. "Where were you all night? I called and called."

"You could have come by."

Kalino's expression grew sheepish. "I did, actually. I saw you and Moke asleep on the lanai. Didn't have the heart to wake you. How are you feeling? Curse removal can absolutely wipe you out."

"Tell me about it. I've been asleep since yesterday. I have no idea how Moke slept without food."

"He didn't. I gave him some dinner." He gave Jack a dazzling smile.

"I had a horrible dream though. I dreamt Moke died."

A slow smile spread across Kalino's face. "You did? But that's wonderful!"

"Wonderful? Are you kidding me?"

"Dreaming of death is very lucky. Especially in Hawaiian culture. It means new beginnings. A deep soul connection. Besides, he's not going anywhere. He's young and healthy and he loves you."

Jack kissed him. "We're lucky to have you, Kalino. Next time, wake me. Wake me with kisses."

Kalino nodded. "I will." He gazed at Jack a moment. "I feel like I waited forever for you to find me. How can I want you so much?" His voice was gruff and sweet.

Jack had no idea, but thought it was somehow poetic and romantic . . . and just so perfect that they should have been adversaries. If this was New York, they'd be in the middle of contentious business dealings.

Instead, Jack soon had Kalino on his back in the middle of his bed, showing him how one New York man liked to take care of business. Especially when it involved his own hot and absolutely perfect, Molokai Man.

"I love you, Jack told him."

"I know. I love you too. Take me to the forest, rainbow man."

And Jack did exactly that. As he slowly undressed the magnificent man in his arms, the thought occurred to him.

Molokai molelo. I myself have heard it.

ABOUT THE AUTHOR

A.J. Llewellyn is the author of over 250 M/M romance novels. She was born in Australia, and lives in Los Angeles. An early obsession with Robinson Crusoe led to a lifelong love affair with islands, particularly Hawaii and Easter Island.

Being marooned once on Wedding Cake Island in Australia cured her of a passion for fishing, but led to a plotline for a novel. A.J.'s friends live in fear because even the smallest details of their lives usually wind up in her stories. A.J. has a desire to paint, draw, juggle, work for the FBI, walk a tightrope with an elephant, be a chess champion, a steeplejack, master chef, and a world-class surfer. She can't do any of these things so she writes about them instead.

A.J. started life as a journalist and boxing columnist, and still enjoys interrogating, er, interviewing people to find out what makes them tick.

How to find/friend me:

email: ajllewellyn@gmail.com
website: www.ajllewellyn.com
www.facebook.com/aj.llewellyn
www.twitter.com/ajllewellyn
Newsletter sign-up: ajllewellynnewsletter@gmail.com—each month I give away a free ebook!
I'm an app! Download my FREE A.J. Llewellyn App for Android here: http://tinyurl.com/lkbc4wm